EXTRAORDINARY*

*the true story of my fairy godparent,
who almost killed me,
and certainly never made me a princess

***the true story of my fairy godparent,
who almost killed me,
and certainly never made me a princess**

ADAM SELZER

Delacorte Press

Text copyright © 2011 by Adam Selzer
Jacket art copyright © 2011 by Mike Heath/Creative Magnus

All rights reserved. Published in the United States by
Delacorte Press, an imprint of Random House Children's Books,
a division of Random House, Inc., New York.

Delacorte Press is a registered trademark and the
colophon is a trademark of Random House, Inc.

Visit us on the Web! www.randomhouse.com/teens

Educators and librarians, for a variety of teaching tools,
visit us at www.randomhouse.com/teachers

Library of Congress Cataloging-in-Publication Data
Selzer, Adam.
Extraordinary : the true story of my fairy godparent, who almost killed me, and certainly never made me a princess / Adam Selzer. — 1st ed.
p. cm.
Summary: Fourteen-year-old Jennifer sets the record straight after a best-selling book, ostensibly written about her, declares that her life was improved by her fairy godparent, who is actually a creepy, unkempt drunk with greasy hair.
ISBN 978-0-385-73649-7 (trade) — ISBN 978-0-385-90612-8 (lib. bdg.) — ISBN 978-0-375-98358-0 (ebook)
[1. Supernatural—Fiction. 2. Fairy godmothers—Fiction. 3. Dating (Social customs)—Fiction. 4. Vampires—Fiction. 5. High schools—Fiction. 6. Schools—Fiction. 7. Family life—Iowa—Fiction. 8. Iowa—Fiction.] I. Title.
PZ7.S4652Ext 2011
[Fic]—dc22
2010046308

The text of this book is set in 12-point Goudy.

Book design by Kenny Holcomb

Printed in the United States of America

10 9 8 7 6 5 4 3 2 1

First Edition

To Ronni,
WHO TOLD ME SHE WAS TIRED OF BOOKS ABOUT
GIRLS WHO THOUGHT THEY'D DIE IF THEY DIDN'T
GO TO THE DANCE. HOPE YOU LIKE THIS ONE!

Acknowledgments

Thanks to Stephanie and Krista, my fantastic editors. Also, thanks to Jennifer Laughran, Taryn Fagerness, Claudia Gray, Kitten McCreery, "The Emily" and the Hamster Trainers, James Kennedy, Colleen Fellingham, Stephanie Kuehnert, and the crews of Sip Coffee and UPS Store #5428 on Grand Avenue.

"Production babies": Maggie Rose and Lola Bel

*the true story of my fairy godparent,
who almost killed me,
and certainly never made me a princess

"So all I have to do is get that boy to kiss me at the dance and I'll be a princess?"

Jenny drew a sharp breath. The air was filled with the smell of daffodils, and the very stars in the sky seemed to be taking on a purple hue. First she'd found out that her naturally purple hair meant she was a fairy, and now she could become a princess, too?

"Just let me take out my wand," said her fairy godmother.

"Jenny Van Den Berg, you were born to be extraordinary. . . ."

—from *Born to Be Extraordinary*, by *New York Times* bestselling author Eileen Codlin

Eileen Codlin sucks cheese.

And I should know. I'm Jennifer Van Den Berg. The real one.

While Eileen is sleeping on mattresses stuffed with money, I get to deal with all the idiots who think I'm *really* a fairy princess and that I can make *other* girls princesses, too, if they just bug me enough.

And with their moms.

Especially their moms.

I'm not a princess. And I don't really *want* to be one. I believe in democracy, and I think it'd be super-awkward to have a servant hanging around me all the time.

But that's only one of a thousand things Eileen changed around for her book to make it more like "what readers want to read." That was nice of her, huh?

When she showed me the first draft, I felt sick to my stomach before I finished the first page.

"So, I guess you're not going to say it was a true story after all, huh?" I asked. "This girl isn't anything like me."

She just laughed. "I want this book to really connect with teens and tweens," she said, "and they probably don't want to be like the *real* you."

Gee, thanks, Eileen. That just makes me feel super.

"If you want to connect with them, stop calling them 'tweens,'" I said. "That's the stupidest word ever."

"But I know what they want," she said, with that stupid fake smile of hers.

"What?" I asked. "Pure crap?"

She just kept on smiling.

But obviously she knew what she was talking about, seeing as how about eleven million people bought the book, and even more saw the movie.

Now, I'm not trying to be mean or spoil your fun or anything, but I feel like I need to clear a few things up.

Also, I need some money.

So this is the real story. Exactly as it happened. I've cleaned up the language in a few places, but that's about it.

First of all, my parents want me to make it very clear that I'm not an orphan. Mom got really upset when she read that she got mowed down by a truck when I was four. Dad wasn't too upset when he read that he was a billionaire playboy who didn't even know I existed, but that's way off, too.

My "fairy godmother" did not smell like daffodils, unless those daffodils were growing in a public restroom that hadn't been cleaned since the early 1980s.

And I know I've been going around saying that Mutual Scrivener, the nerd who keeps trying to kiss me in the book, is a fictional character, but, well . . . you'll see.

And here's fair warning: if it's crap you want, well, you're gonna get it. The real story has a lot more unicorn poop in it than the version you've already read. Just, a *lot* more. *Born to Be Extraordinary* didn't mention that stuff at all, which is probably just as well, but I can't tell the real story without it.

To be fair, though, Eileen did get *some* things right.

When the story began, I really was a normal, smart, slightly chubby but totally lovable (most of the time) teenage girl from Iowa.

I do have purple hair (though I wasn't born with it or anything—it's dyed). I also have purple clothes, purple walls in my bedroom, and anything else purple that I can get. I'm purpliferous. And yes, that's a real word (especially now that it's in a book).

And I do have a friend named Amber. She's really awesome, too.

The guy you've seen in pictures with me isn't really Fred, but Fred was a real guy. He was really a vampire, too.

And the story of my fairy godmother really did start out on a lousy, crappy, soul-sucking, butt-sniffing, very bad day.

Jenny climbed out of her Prius and waved to Melinda Cranston's mom, who was sitting on the porch with Melinda. Melinda was crying already. It was going to be another long piano lesson.

As Jenny walked up the driveway, Melinda's little brother threw a pair of dirty underpants out his window, narrowly missing Jenny's head.

If only I were a princess, she thought, *I wouldn't have to teach piano to these brats just to make my car payments!*

one

I think "Jenny" must have had a second job holding up convenience stores. Take it from me, you do *not* earn enough money teaching piano to buy a Prius.

It's true that I taught piano, but my real car, the Jenmobile, was an old powder-blue thing that looked like it couldn't decide whether it was a sedan or a station wagon. I bought it at an auction for two hundred fifty dollars, and I probably overpaid. There were over three hundred thousand miles on the odometer, it had a weird smell that I could never get rid of, and it stalled more than a six-year-old at bedtime.

When it stalled on the way to school that fateful November morning, I patted the dashboard and said, "Come on, baby. It's just a few more blocks."

Sometimes that got it to start back up right away. This time it didn't.

It almost always started back up if I just gave it five or ten minutes, but the heater wouldn't come on when the car was stalled, and there was freezing rain coming down that morning. I wasn't about to sit there in the cold, so I put on the flashers, braved the sleet, and ran down Cedar Avenue to McDonald's for a cup of coffee.

That was where the story began.

When I stepped inside, a gruff voice called out, "Hoo hoo!" and I turned to see a scruffy guy sitting at a table wearing a tattered overcoat and a bent fedora.

"Excuse me?" I asked.

"Anyone ever tell you you look like Grimace, kiddo?" he asked.

"Who?"

He flashed me a goblin grin and stood up. When he did, I saw that he was hunchbacked, and couldn't have been more than four and a half feet tall. His curly brown hair—what I could see of it under his hat—must have been at least 50 percent grease.

The little weirdo hobbled up to a sign on the wall with all the characters from the McDonald's commercials and pointed at Grimace: the big, fat purple guy who looked like a talking eggplant or something.

"All that purple you got on, kiddo," he said, in a growly voice that made it sound like he was gargling whiskey. "You're the spitting image!"

For a second I was too dumbstruck to say anything.

He was the one who looked like something made by Jim Henson's Creature Shop. And he was calling *me* a big, fat eggplant man.

"Dick," I said.

He kept grinning at me as I slunk away from him and walked up to the counter.

My purple coat made me look fat. That was all. It was a big coat. I knew I wasn't the skinniest person in town or anything, but I was *not* shaped like an eggplant.

"Don't mind him," the woman at the register whispered. "He's been here every day lately. And when we close, we see him sitting in the parking lot across the street, smoking cigars."

"What a freak," I said.

"And when he gets a burger, he eats the whole thing. Like, the wrapper and everything."

I looked back over at the guy. He was back to sitting at his table, pouring some red liquid from a bottle in a brown bag into a teaspoon and slurping it up. I assumed it was not grape juice.

He was not the kind of guy you expect to see in Iowa. Not in suburban Des Moines, anyway. Maybe out in the smaller towns. There are plenty of weirdos out there. I ought to know—my town used to *be* a small town before it got absorbed into suburbia, and it was a regular freak show.

"Maybe you should call the cops," I said. "Are you sure he didn't, like, escape from an asylum or something?"

"No!" the weirdo shouted from his table. "I didn't."

I blushed and probably shivered a bit. I hadn't thought he could possibly hear us.

He put the bottle away, looked out the window at the strip malls and sleet, and started singing a song that went "Bang, bang, Lulu, bang away strong . . ."

"Well," I whispered, "you could at least get him on public drunkenness."

"Believe me, we've tried." The woman sighed. "But he passes the test every time."

When I left, I gave the guy my dirtiest look for his Grimace remark, but he didn't acknowledge me. He just kept singing to the window.

As I walked back to my car, I imagined three creative ways to murder him for calling me fat: dropping heavy rocks on his head; carving him into a funny shape with a chain saw; and tying a rope around his feet, swinging him around above my head, and throwing him clear to Omaha.

Then I poured my coffee into the gutter, put the empty cup on the ground, and stomped on it.

I liked to break things in those days.

Now, don't get me wrong—I wasn't some violent maniac or anything. All things considered, I was fairly well adjusted. I didn't even kill bugs if I could help it.

But up through the end of my junior year, my workload was about eighty hours per week, between school and various extracurriculars my parents made me do to pad my college applications. The only way I stayed sane was by reading a whole lot of Shakespeare (which I swear makes you breathe better) and squeezing in an hour or two a week to hang out with Jason and Amber, my best friends.

Still, friends and Shakespeare couldn't keep me from getting stressed out now and then, and nothing relieved stress like breaking stuff.

Little porcelain angels from the dollar store were the best. Man, do those things shatter.

But at the end of junior year, I got early acceptance through a special program at Drake, which is sort of the Harvard of Des Moines. The extracurriculars and volunteer work and advanced classes were no longer necessary, so I gave myself a *much* lighter schedule for my senior year. Breaking stuff was hardly a part of my life anymore.

I was expecting this to be a really good day. My math class would be stuff I'd learned years ago. I could snooze through English while people read out loud from *The Canterbury Tales* at a rate of three words per minute. Debate would just be listening to the underclassmen argue about whether the new T-shirts should say "We Kick Rebuttal" or "We're *Master* Debaters."

And in drama, I'd just be relaxing while the cast rehearsed *The Music Man*. I was working props, a job that so far required me to do nothing more than sit on my butt and watch the rehearsals.

But the day started to fall apart the minute the Jenmobile stalled, and it only got worse from there.

In addition to being told that I look like a giant eggplant by a pint-sized, burger-wrapper-eating freak, I realized later that morning that I'd left my lunch sitting on the kitchen table.

Then I slammed my fingers in my locker.

And when I got to the *Music Man* rehearsal in fourth period, Cathy Marconi, one of the handful of people I *didn't* get along with, kept staring at me, smirking. I was just starting to wonder if *she'd* noticed that I looked like Grimace, too, when the doors swung open and a familiar gruff voice shouted out, "Hoo hoo!"

Oh. God.

I looked behind me to see the weirdo from McDonald's standing in the doorway between the hall and the auditorium.

"Ah!" he shouted. "This joint ain't the Palace, but it'll do!"

Everyone turned and watched as he strutted down the aisle like he owned the place. He hoisted himself onto the stage, and I slumped down in my seat, praying he wouldn't see me and make another Grimace remark.

"Who are you?" someone asked.

He stood up as straight as he could and took a bow.

"My name is Gregory Grue," he said. "I'm your new director!"

I slumped a bit farther down.

"What about Mrs. Alison?" asked Cathy, who was playing Eulalie Shinn, the mayor's wife.

Gregory smiled. "I'm afraid she'll be taking a leave of absence," he said.

"Did they finally find out that her water bottle was full of vodka?" someone asked.

"I don't wish to comment on the particulars, or lend credence to malicious gossip that happens to be true," said Gregory. "The important thing is that she's gone and I'm here, with a nail in my shoe and a song in my heart."

"Do you know anything about theater?" asked Cathy.

Gregory laughed. His laugh sounded like a lawn mower trying to start.

"I studied at the RSC for three years," he said. "Any of you little punks know what that stands for?"

My jaw dropped as someone a row ahead of me called out "Royal Shakespeare Company." Gregory Grue grinned and nodded.

I had been a Shakespeare fanatic since I was nine, so I knew that the Royal Shakespeare Company was just about the most famous Shakespeare troupe in the world. And as much as I hated to think anything good about this guy after what he'd said to me that morning, I could totally picture him playing Iago or Richard the Third.

In fact, just as I was thinking that, he waved his hand with a theatrical flourish and went into Richard's opening monologue.

> "Now is the winter of our discontent
> Made glorious summer by this sun of York;
> And all the clouds that lour'd upon our house
> In the deep bosom of the ocean buried."

He said that in a much clearer voice than his normal one; for a second, it was like he really did become Richard. It was enough to see that this guy was a damned good actor.

"Just like how the winter of *your* discontent is about to be made glorious summer by Gregory Grue!" he said. "I've never directed a high school show before, but if I can get through three years with the RSC, I think I can handle a musical about a traveling salesman who cons a bunch of Iowans. Everyone get in your places, and we'll run through the 'Wells Fargo Wagon' number so I can see where your strengths and weaknesses are. Then I'll yell at you until you don't have any weaknesses left."

And while I sat and watched, he started to direct people. He seemed to know what he was doing, but I couldn't stop thinking that he seemed . . . creepy. Every now and then he would look over at me and grin, leaving me scared to death that he was going to make some other comment about my weight right in front of everyone.

I wasn't used to comments about my weight back then, and hadn't made peace with the fact that I had inherited my mother's slightly round body type. I've sort of had to get used to it now that I'm kind of famous and people think they can say whatever horrible thing they want about me on Internet forums, but it was still pretty new to me at the time.

So when Kyle, the office messenger, walked into the room and told me that the principal, Mr. Jablonski, and the guidance counselor, Mrs. Smollet, wanted to see me, I didn't argue. I would have taken any excuse to get away from Gregory, even though I didn't much care for having to talk to Mrs. Smollet. The woman was pretty scary herself. She was a vampire, after all. And not one of the nicer ones, either.

No hair dye would stick to Jenny's hair—no matter what she did, it always stayed purple. This drove Jenny crazy—she wanted *so* badly to have hair as black as ebony, and skin as white as snow. All the other girls in her class had dyed their hair black the same week they found out that vampires were real.

two

Actually, by the time I was a senior, vampires had been "out of the coffin" for six years, and the whole "going goth so the vampires will like me" thing was pretty much over.

We'd all gotten used to having them around, for the most part. Most of them seemed like nice, regular people who just happened to be really strong, able to run a thousand miles per hour, and immune to aging. They hadn't had to drink blood since the Civil War, when someone developed a vegetable compound that was even more satisfying, so they were no real threat.

But they weren't *all* nice.

Victorian vampires—the ones who converted in the eighteen hundreds—are usually the worst. People in the seventeen hundreds were fairly wild and crazy, but in the eighteen hundreds the world went through a sort of prudish phase. Vampires from back then never quite got used to living in a world where women dressed in outfits that showed their ankles.

Mrs. Smollet, the guidance counselor, was one of those. She was cold and creepy, the kind of vampire who just reinforced all the worst stereotypes.

Kyle the messenger led me down the hall.

"Do you know what they want?" I asked.

Kyle shrugged. "Probably just for you to fill out a form."

"How've you been, anyway?" I asked. "I haven't seen you since I quit working in the office."

"Same as ever," he said. "You still in the running for valedictorian?"

"Not that I know of," I said. "I'm already accepted at Drake, as long as I don't flunk out or anything, so I'm not really worrying about that stuff anymore."

"Nice."

God, it *was* nice not to have to worry about my class rank. Some might call it senioritis, but I called it a necessary step toward preserving my mental health.

Kyle had me sit down on one of the chairs in front of the secretary's desk, then disappeared on some other errand.

The door to the principal's office opened and Mr. Jablonski poked his head out.

"Miss Van Den Berg?" he asked.

"Here I am."

He motioned me into his office. Mrs. Smollet was standing there behind his desk with her arms crossed, like I was trespassing in her lair or something.

My ice skates were sitting on Mr. Jablonski's desk.

"Hey!" I said. "Did you guys break into my locker?"

"So they're yours?" Jablonski asked. "No one planted them there to set you up?"

"Yeah," I said. "I'm hoping the storm will put enough ice on the sidewalk that I can skate home."

When I saw that we were getting the first freezing rain of the year, I'd packed my ice skates. Odds that I'd actually be able to skate home were slim to none, but I thought I'd give it a shot. Jason and Amber had already agreed to follow me and give me a ride if I couldn't make it.

Smollet eyed me skeptically.

"You were going to skate clear from Cornersville back to Preston?"

My town had grown up a lot since I was a kid, but the high school wasn't finished being built yet, so I had to commute. It probably *was* a lot farther than I could possibly have skated, but I wasn't about to admit that to Smollet.

"I was going to have help from my friends," I said.

Mr. Jablonski looked over at Mrs. Smollet like he was going to say something, but she just glared at him. I swear he shuddered.

"Jennifer," said Mr. Jablonski, "the blades on these skates are very sharp."

"Sure," I said.

"Having objects like these in your locker is a violation of the school board's zero-tolerance policy on deadly weapons," said Mrs. Smollet.

"You have to be kidding me," I said.

Mr. Jablonski shook his head. "I'm afraid not. And we have to take that zero-tolerance policy very seriously."

I knew he meant it. I'd seen kids get in trouble over

having plastic wrap rubber-banded over stuff in their lunch, because rubber bands can be used as projectiles.

But I also knew that the board tended to be very random in terms of how they actually *enforced* that rule. I could get out of this. Jablonski looked nervous already.

I summoned all my old debate team skills and got ready for a fight. I was good at debate. I could have become a lawyer, if I wanted to give up my soul.

"Taking those skates from my locker without a warrant constitutes illegal search and seizure," I said.

"Locker searches are perfectly legal," Jablonski said with a sigh. "There's a thing about it in the handbook."

"I think the Fourth Amendment to the U.S. Constitution trumps the Cornersville Trace High School handbook."

"Sorry, Jennifer," said Jablonski. "Lockers are school property, not student property. We can search them all we want. Trust me, we've been through this mill with the stoners a few times."

There went my first defense.

"We have to take all threats seriously, Miss Van Den Berg," Smollet said. "And Cathy Marconi told us she was afraid you were planning to attack her again."

I felt the blood rush to my face.

I should have known it was her. That explained the smirk.

"Then I object to the language of her accusation," I said. "She's implying that I've attacked her *before*, and I haven't."

"You broke her nose two years ago," said Mrs. Smollet.

"That was a volleyball accident, not an attack," I said.

Cathy used to work at the dollar store where Jason and Amber and I would go to buy stuff for me to destroy when I got stressed, so she had never quite believed it was an accident when I spiked a volleyball into her face. She'd seen what I did to those little porcelain trinkets out in the parking lot.

"Okay," Jablonski said. "I'll sustain your objection. But the fact stands. She thought her safety was at risk, and we found contraband materials in your locker. It's an automatic in-school suspension."

I had never been suspended before, and I didn't want to start now.

I was going to have to play hardball.

"Come on," I said. "You let people who have been seventeen for decades go to school here. I'm sure I don't have to remind you of the events of three years ago."

"That was an isolated incident," Smollet said. "And you know what the Council of Elders did to Wilhelm."

"His clan vowed revenge," I said.

"They've also been banished to the Yukon Territory."

You've probably already heard about the events I was talking about—when Wilhelm, a vampire from my school, attacked a girl named Alley and her zombie boyfriend, Doug, at the prom. They were only saved when feral zombies attacked.

It was a pretty messed-up prom.

"Fine," I said. "But vampires are still more dangerous than ice skates, if you break it down to empirical evidence. Vampires have attacked a student at this school, and they could get here on foot from the Yukon in an hour and a half. I don't think there's ever been an ice skate attack."

I wanted to add "You just got lawyered, bee-yotch," but I wasn't stupid.

And frankly, I felt like a dick just making that argument. It's the same argument bigoted jerks use when they say vampires should have to sit at the back of the bus or whatever.

And I don't believe that at all—I'm a member of the Iowa Human/Post-Human Alliance. It's one of the activities I kept going to even when I dropped most of the other ones. I totally support post-human rights.

But part of being a good debater is being able to argue for a side you don't really agree with.

"Sorry, Jennifer," said Jablonski. "It's automatic, even if I do think this whole thing is ridiculous myself. I'm only going to keep you in the in-school suspension room for the rest of the day, but I can't do any less than that."

Mrs. Smollet stepped forward and motioned for me to follow her. I had lost.

This day just kept getting worse.

I followed her through the office, where Kyle gave me a consolation sigh, and into the little in-school suspension room. I sat down in a chair that must have been on loan from a preschool—my whole butt didn't fit into it, which didn't exactly help me feel less like a human eggplant.

For most of the next hour, I had nothing to do but sit there, stew about the size of my butt, and imagine Cathy, Mrs. Smollet, and Gregory Grue being in the same plane crash over the Atlantic. It wouldn't kill Mrs. Smollet, but getting back to dry land would at least be a major inconvenience for her.

I wouldn't be ice-skating home after all.

I really had wanted to try that, too.

Ever since I was a kid, I'd had this idea of the kind of person I wanted to be. I thought of myself as one of those women you always see in old screwball comedies—the kind who have pet leopards, keep their undies in the freezer, and walk barefoot through the park in January. They operate on a sort of internal logic that makes people think they're crazy—until it turns out that they're the smartest characters in the movie.

But my eighty-hour-a-week schedule had never left me much time to try my hand at being a teenage Pippi Longstocking. Now that I finally had some free time, I wanted to get started on being more . . . well, being more extraordinary (something I really wish I hadn't told Eileen about).

But so far, all I had really done was dye my hair purple. I *meant* to go write poetry in coffee shops, dance naked in front of windows, and all that, but I'd usually get wrapped up in looking things up online, and, well . . . you know how it is. I still felt as ordinary as ever. Ice-skating home from school had seemed like just the kind of thing that would kick-start my career as a free-spirited eccentric.

The day was almost over when Mrs. Smollet came back, with Jason and Amber marching behind her.

My face brightened and Jason gave me a triumphant grin.

"I have some company for you, Miss Van Den Berg," said Smollet.

"What are you guys doing here?" I asked.

"They caught us burning stuff," Jason said casually.

He tossed his backpack across the room. Smollet vanished for a second, then reappeared in front of him, holding it. She'd done that vampire trick where they run so fast you can't even see them—it looks like they're just vanishing and reappearing.

"Watch yourselves," she said, handing it back to him.

"You're locking me into a room with a couple of pyros," I said. "Concerned about safety, my butt."

"And your mouths," she said.

This is *not* one of the parts of the book where I'm cleaning up the language. Victorian vampires always think words like "butt" are swear words.

But scaring old ladies has been a hobby of Jason's as long as I could remember, and Mrs. Smollet was an easy target.

"No telling what we might get up to," said Jason. "A boy and two girls in a room together . . . with our loose modern morals . . . anything could happen!"

"Mass-teria!" I said.

"Don't think I won't be watching," Smollet said. "No funny business."

I blinked, and she was gone.

Jason, Amber, and I looked at each other, then started to laugh.

I felt a million times better just being in the same room with the two of them. I was still mad at Cathy and Mrs. Smollet and Gregory Grue, but having Jason and Amber there gave me something to do besides sulk.

"We heard about what happened to you from Kyle," said Jason. "And I had to see it for myself. Jennifer Van Den Berg, every teacher's favorite student ever, in trouble!"

"You guys got yourselves in trouble just for me?" I asked.

"We couldn't let a chance like this go by," said Amber as she slipped her hand into Jason's. "The three of us haven't all been in trouble together in years!"

"I was overdue for some trouble anyway," said Jason. "If I don't keep my eyes on the prize, they won't rename this room the Jason Keyes Memorial In-School Suspension Room when I graduate."

I smiled and gave him a high five.

Only a few people from my old one-class-per-grade elementary school in Preston were still at Cornersville Trace High with me, but I felt like we'd been through a war together. Especially Jason and Amber. Even though they were a couple of metalheads and I was more into show tunes and Renaissance fair–type music, we just had a sort of bond.

Jason always prided himself on being a no-good kid; on his eighteenth birthday, he got a tattoo that said "Bad for Good" on his butt and showed it to everyone who was brave enough to look. And plenty of old ladies who weren't.

But he wasn't *really* bad. He was a badass when he had to be, but he was one of the nicest guys I'd ever met. He wasn't mean at all. He just liked burning stuff and frightening old ladies. That was about all there was to do in Preston when we were kids, back before they built the mall and the rest of suburbia caught up to us.

"So what're you in for, exactly?" Jason asked.

"Deadly weapons," I said.

"No way!" he said. "You? Weapons?"

"It was the ice skates," I said. "Cathy said she was afraid I was going to cut her with them."

Amber groaned. "You have got to be kidding me."

I shook my head. "Hadn't occurred to me before, but now I'd sort of like to cut her from nave to chops."

"Cool," Jason said. "Do girls have naves?"

" 'Nave' means 'navel,' " I said. " ' 'Nave to chops' is 'belly button to jaw.' It's a Shakespeare thing."

"Cool," Jason said, again. "You *would* know that."

I smiled.

"How 'bout you guys?" I asked. "What did you burn?"

"Nothing much," Amber said. "Just the cover of Jason's science book."

"They said we could either pay for it or do a stint in in-school," he said. "This is cheaper. I did them a favor, if you ask me. That thing was ten years old. Every bio book from before the vampires showed up is out of date now."

"Totally," I said. "It's just a shame you didn't throw Marconi in the fire while you were at it."

And I imagined a tiny version of Cathy in the little grill in the picnic area, her flesh blistering and turning black while she screamed.

Then I told them all about Gregory Grue, the little weirdo who had called me fat at McDonald's, and Amber hugged me and told me never to mind what idiots thought.

"*Illegitimis non carborundum,*" she said. "That's Latin for 'Don't let the bastards grind you down.' Is tonight your alliance meeting?"

I nodded.

"With that guy from Valley?"

I nodded again and blushed.

The only other teenager in the Iowa Human/Post-Human Alliance was a guy from West Des Moines named Corey Tapley. I wouldn't have gone so far as to call him my crush, but he and I had been flirting back and forth for months, and homecoming *was* just around the corner.

"Then you can still salvage the day. Think he's gonna ask you out?"

I shrugged. "I don't know," I said. "It's not like I'm in love with him or anything. I'd just kind of like to *go* to a dance before I graduate."

"Well, ask *him*, then," said Amber.

"I don't know if I have the guts for that," I said.

"Sure you do," she said. "You *deserve* to have a better day than this."

I smiled again.

Amber had a real talent for making me feel brave. I never would have had the nerve to swear at Mrs. Smollet—even just using the word "butt"—without her in the room.

I was actually starting to feel halfway decent by the end of the day, but when the last bell rang, Mrs. Smollet escorted us through the halls to the back door, and Cathy was standing at her locker grinning at me.

Fred, her vampire boyfriend, was kissing her neck and running his fingers through her hair. As we passed by, she gave me a smug "ha-ha, I win" look. The kind of look that made me want to spray toxic acid all over her.

She had probably made a point of being where I'd see her getting kissed to emphasize the fact that no one ever kissed *me* in the hallway.

I tried to run up to her and give her a good yelling-at, but Smollet ushered me right past her and said, "Stay away from her, Jennifer. Let it go."

I kept walking and imagined Cathy falling into a grain silo and either drowning or breaking her neck—whichever it is that happens when you fall into those.

For the record, I don't *like* to have fantasies like that. I don't believe in violence in real life. Seriously.

But when I'm having a lousy, crappy, soul-sucking, butt-sniffing, very bad day, I can't help thinking about chopping annoying people to bits and then pouring what's left of them down a storm drain into a sewer. It just makes me feel better sometimes. It helps me break all the bad feelings down into smaller pieces that can be filed away for later, when I can relieve all the stress by breaking stuff.

The look on Cathy's face haunted me all the way home.

By the time the Jenmobile got me back to Preston (which took half an hour, since it stalled out twice), the annoyance had turned into a slow-burning rage that was going to need to be dealt with.

I took three porcelain angel figurines out of the box under my bed and smashed them to smithereens on the icy sidewalk in front of my house, imagining that one of them was Cathy, one of them was Mrs. Smollet, and one of them was Gregory Grue. I loved the weight of the hammer in my hand, the satisfying crash it made when it came down on the porcelain, the *plink* sound when it hit the sidewalk—or, in this case, the *crack* when it busted the thin layer of ice.

I was still cleaning up the broken pieces when I looked up and saw that the Wells Fargo Wagon was coming down my street.

Jenny sighed as she stood behind the piano, practicing singing one of her songs for the school musical.

"I'm never going to get this!" she said sadly. "I couldn't hit that note if I stood on a chair!"

"Keep trying," said Amber. "I know you can do it. You're going to be a star!"

Jenny tried again. She felt so lucky to have someone like Amber—a popular, skinny girl who always had the very latest shoes and knew all the latest music—as a friend.

three

One thing I'll say for Eileen: she nailed Amber.

Well, in a way. The real Amber is about my size and wears fishnets and pentagram necklaces. And she listens to metal, not pop, like the book version of her. She certainly wasn't "popular," exactly.

But she did wear the very latest footwear—her shoes were always *that* season's ten-dollar Converse knockoffs. And she really was a friend I was lucky to have.

I didn't play Marian the Librarian in *The Music Man*, like "Jenny" does, but if I had, Amber would have helped me and encouraged me and made me feel braver, just like she does in the book.

And if I'd really been practicing my singing, maybe I would have been less pitchy when I sang out the "Wells Fargo Wagon" song on my lawn upon seeing one coming down my street.

Now, in case you've never seen *The Music Man*, it's all about this con artist named Professor Harold Hill. He's a traveling salesman back in 1912 who goes from small town to small town convincing parents that their sons are going to grow up to be immoral bums, then offers to solve the problem by teaching the kids to play musical instruments and organizing them into a band. But he doesn't really know a thing about music; as soon as he collects the money for the instruments and uniforms, he skips town, never to be seen again, leaving the townspeople with a bunch of instruments they can't play while he goes off to pull the same con in another town.

Since it takes place here in Iowa, every high school drama department does it every now and then. We Iowans love anything with Iowa in it (pronounce Des Moines correctly—like *"Duh Moyne"*—on television and we'll love you forever), so even the crappiest of high school productions is likely to sell enough tickets to break even.

And when I say the Wells Fargo Wagon was coming down my street, I mean a *Wells Fargo Wagon*. Like, the old horse-drawn kind they sing about in the show at the end of act one, when it rolls into town with all the junk people ordered from catalogs. But instead of a horse, this one was being led by a tow truck that came down my street and turned right into my driveway.

When the door to the tow truck opened, I just about fainted.

The driver was Gregory Grue.

He was wearing a jumpsuit that looked like it was supposed to be white, but it was practically tie-dyed with stains.

"Hoo hoo!" he said. "I see you're hammering out love between your brothers and sisters all over this land."

I tried to keep calm as well as I could.

"You're a delivery man, too?" I asked.

He chuckled. "I don't know much about economics," he said, "but I do know that you can't make a living teaching one class a day. And ladies love a man who delivers the goods!"

"I thought the techies were *building* the Wells Fargo Wagon," I said.

"Nope," he said. "They can't. You need all kinds of tools that violate the zero-tolerance weapons policy to build something like this. They ordered it from a prop supplier."

I sighed. "I believe that," I said. "But why don't you just take it over to the school? I can't do anything with it here."

He shrugged. "The sheet says to deliver it *here*, so I can't take it *there*. Sign here, madam."

He held out a form on a clipboard and I signed it.

"I'll put in a request at the school to have it towed there," he said, "but it'll take a while."

He left the wagon in the driveway, then jumped up into his truck, gave me a little salute, and drove off singing "*It's a long way to Cornersville Trace, it's a long way to go. . . .*"

When the tow truck was gone, the wagon looked like some sort of billboard for the Wells Fargo company in my driveway. They should have paid me.

And it's not too late. Hint hint.

I told myself I'd probably been seeing Gregory around for years but never noticed him, because he had never called me

Grimace before. It was like when you learn a new word and suddenly hear it three times the next day.

At least he didn't eat the form I'd signed or anything. As far as I knew. There was no telling what he did with it once he got back into the truck.

I finished cleaning up the debris I'd created and shook off the general feeling of creepiness Gregory gave me just in time for Melinda Cranston's mom to drop her off for her piano lesson.

I did, in fact, teach Melinda piano, like "Jenny" does in Eileen's book. But she came to my house, not the other way around, so if she *did* have a little brother, he never threw any underwear at me (thank God). And Eileen was at least nice enough not to mention that I was probably the world's least competent piano teacher. I'd taken flute, piano, and violin just long enough to list them on a college application, and I'd be out of a job as soon as Melinda got through the advanced beginner workbook.

Luckily for me, at the rate she was going, that would take a while. She wasn't as bratty as the girl in the book, but she was not what you'd call a gifted musician.

Midway through her fifth attempt at playing "The Animal Band," my parents came charging into the living room—both at once, which was odd, since I'd hardly ever seen them together since the divorce.

"Okay," said Mom. "Your side, please."

"Can this wait?" I asked. "I'm working."

"Melinda," said Mom, "work on your cross-hand piece. We need to talk to Jennifer in the kitchen."

I hated it when she butted in when I was trying to

teach—it undermined my role as the teacher, which could only stand up to so much undermining to begin with. But I got off the bench and followed them to the kitchen.

"So I guess Jablonski called you," I said as we walked out of the living room and into the kitchen.

They nodded just as Melinda hit the wrong key on the piano.

"What in the heck were you thinking, taking skates to school?" asked Dad. "If the principal hadn't suspended you, Cathy could have gone to the press and accused him of being tolerant of deadly weapons, and he could have lost his job."

"I thought it would be fun to try to ice-skate home, since it was going to be icy," I said.

Then I turned toward the living room to shout "Use both hands, Melinda! That's why they call it cross-hand!"

"You would have gotten stranded halfway and missed the piano lesson and lost *your* job," said Dad.

"Jason and Amber were going to follow me to make sure I made it in time."

"Relax, Mitchell, she would have been fine," said Mom. "Now, can we just get down to dealing with this?"

Dad wasn't done.

"You only wanted people to see you skating and think about what a nonconformist you must be," he went on.

"No!"

"First the purple hair, and now this."

"Like anyone in school still has their natural hair color, Dad. *Melinda* doesn't have her natural hair color."

"Right," said Dad.

When the guy playing Harold Hill did a crappy job in

rehearsal, Mrs. Alison would say, "Try that again—I didn't quite *believe* you that time." Sometimes I think my whole attempt to become a charming eccentric came off like a crappy rehearsal. Dad sure didn't believe it.

Mom is fairly sane, as parents go, but I always sort of wished my dad really *were* a jet-set type who was never around to embarrass me with his lousy attempts to make me into an overachiever, which were known to include espionage, bribery, and possibly some light treason. Growing up with him had forced me to become an expert at compartmentalizing—pushing unpleasant things from the front of my mind into their own little compartments—which can really come in handy. I don't know if I could have survived this whole story without it.

For instance, while he whined about my hair, I decided to stop focusing on him and focus on something else: food. I reached into the pantry, grabbed a jar of peanut butter, and started eating right out of the damned thing.

There was definitely no way I could start my new, free-spirited life, the one I'd always wanted, while I lived in a house to which he still had keys.

"Now we need to get on the phone with Drake," he said with a sigh, "and make sure this doesn't affect your scholarships or anything."

"Why would it?" I asked.

"Getting suspended?" said Dad. "You don't think that makes you less attractive to a college? They took a chance by giving you early acceptance as it was. You'll be lucky to get into the Shaker Heights Institute of Technology now."

"Two hands, Melinda!" I shouted again.

"But it's hard!" she shouted back.

"It's supposed to be!"

"I'll call them," said Mom, "but I'm sure it's fine."

While Mom got out a list of phone numbers, I imagined grinding Cathy Marconi into peanut butter in some kind of enormous peanut butter–making machine, then spreading her onto pinecones and covering her with birdseed at a Girl Scout Jamboree.

If the suspension made Drake start to think twice, I'd probably have to pick up more extracurriculars to get back in to their good graces. I didn't have time for that. Becoming an extraordinary person takes practice, just like a cross-hand piano piece, and I felt like I had my work cut out for me.

"I suppose we should probably be grounding you," said Mom.

"For the rest of the year," added Dad.

"Please don't," I said. "I need to go to the alliance meeting tonight."

Mom and Dad looked at each other.

"It really was just a technicality," Mom said.

"A technicality that could cost her her entire future!" said Dad.

"Oh, please." Mom looked over at me. "They aren't going to screw up her future over a third-of-the-day suspension, Mitchell. You weren't really thinking of attacking Cathy, right, Jennifer?"

I shook my head. "Not seriously."

"Then just promise you're not going to the meeting tonight to get someone on the vampire Council of Elders to have Mrs. Smollet torn to bits, okay?"

"Done," I said.

It wasn't like anyone from the Council of Elders would even be there. It's called the Iowa Human/Post-Human Alliance, but only a handful of actual post-humans ever came. This is Des Moines, after all. We're not really known for diversity here to start with, and about half the vampires in town had moved away to a place where people would be less suspicious of their every move after Alley got attacked.

"Now can I get back to work?"

"Okay," Mom said. "You can go."

She nodded, and I sat back down at the piano bench just in time to hit a key Melinda was about to miss.

Some of you might have met Dad. He's the guy in the three-piece suit who comes by now and then—even though it's not his house anymore—and turns the hose on the people who camp out on the lawn.

And don't bother trying to sue. You can be on my sidewalk, but once you set foot on my lawn, anything we do is nice and legal.

Trust me. I've checked.

"Just act natural," Amber said sneakily. "Vampires like girls who act natural."

"But this black wig itches!" said Jenny hopelessly. "I'll never be able to keep it on!"

They crept through the back window into the armory, where all the vampires in town were meeting with the mayor, the local news anchors, and all the other members of the Iowa Human/Post-Human Alliance, the glitziest charity in town.

Jenny was sure Amber would be walking out with a post-human date to the dance, and equally sure that she herself would be spending the dance watching TV and eating ice cream—as usual.

four

There was no need to sneak into the Iowa Human/Post-Human Alliance meetings. The ones at the armory building were open to the public, and there were always empty seats. It wasn't any more glamorous than most flea markets.

Inside, Eileen Codlin was the first person I saw.

"Jenny V!" she said. "How are you tonight?"

"Hi, Eileen," I said, as politely as I could. I don't know where she got the idea that I went by "Jenny." I did not. Nor do I now. But it's all she ever called me, either in person or in her book.

Back then, I knew Eileen as a flaky woman from the alliance who was always going around talking about some book she was working on; it was going to be some sort of encyclopedia of post-humans, including stuff like gnomes and the Loch Ness Monster that probably weren't even real. She was one of a large number of people who assumed that since vampires and zombies *were* real, so was everything *else* she'd ever read about in a fantasy novel.

I never believed the rumors that she was on meth, but I didn't take her very seriously. No one did. I wouldn't have sold her the rights to my story for a lousy five hundred bucks if I thought she could *actually* make a book out of it.

But I tried to be polite to her, like always.

"How's your book coming?" I asked.

"Oh, wonderful," she said. "I'm taking care of some magical creatures for research. I'm getting a gryphon next week!"

"Cool," I said, trying to sound like I believed she was really going to get a gryphon, not just a cat that someone had glued feathers onto. "Will you excuse me for a second?"

A group of people were crowded around Murray, one of our two or three token vampires. I crept away from Eileen, tossed my coat onto a table with everyone else's, and headed over to see what was happening.

In the middle of the group, Murray was holding up his phone to show a video of a new Megamart commercial, which showed a smiling zombie talking about how grateful he was that Megamart had "given him the gift of life" when they raised up his corpse to work as slave labor in their stockrooms.

"See," said Murray, in his New York accent. "What a bunch of dirtbags."

"That's just what we don't need," I said. "Another Igor on television."

"Igor" is what we call zombies who act like Megamart is really a terrific operation for enslaving them. They make people think that we don't *need* to give zombies any rights, because they're happier without them.

"It's probably not even a real zombie," someone said. "If I know Megamart, they just got some guy to put on zombie makeup."

"The minstrel show of the post-human era," said Murray.

I loved hearing Murray talk. He sounded like an agent for a Broadway singer or something. That kind of accent is a total novelty around here.

"Did you ever go to one of those, back in the day?" I asked.

Murray blushed a little.

"You can admit it," I said with a chuckle. "You guys didn't know any better back then."

He smiled a tiny bit and took a deep breath. "Anyone who lives from era to era ends up doing stuff they ain't proud of," he said. "At least I know better now. I'm not like one of them Victorians."

Everyone nodded and patted him on the back. Except for a Victorian vampire, who kind of scowled.

Murray was one of my favorite vampires, partly because he dealt with changing times better than most of them. So many vampires still thought that "vampire culture" gave them a free pass to act like total douchebags. These are the ones who defend all the pressure they put on the children of vampires to convert by saying "That's just what vampires do."

Worst. Excuse. Ever.

But you can't really blame them—if they weren't that forward-thinking or open-minded when they became vampires, they probably never would be. When you don't age, your brain doesn't really evolve.

See, this was the kind of stuff we discussed at the alliance. We talked about post-human rights, whether vampire teenagers should be in schools, and whether executing post-human convicts counted as the death penalty, since they were technically already dead. It wasn't anything like the glamorous vampire social club Eileen made it out to be. It was the kind of place where you threw your coat on a table and hoped the radiator was working that night.

I felt a tap on my shoulder and turned to see Corey Tapley, in all his skinny, dreadlocked glory.

"Hi," he said.

"Hi," I said, giving him the sexiest smile I could.

Corey was a lanky guy who sort of looked like a blond Ichabod Crane. He was much more of a hard-core activist type than I was—he was always going to protests and rallies, usually for stuff I thought was pretty pointless. But we got along really well anyway. I wasn't exactly *attracted* to him, but there was always a chance that a romantic evening at a dance could win me over.

"What's been going on?" he asked.

I told him the whole thing about getting suspended, and he groaned in the right places. But then he started talking about how we should get some picket signs made up and organize a big protest against the school's weapons policy. Like that would work. I just smiled and nodded most of the time when he talked, and this was no exception.

We sat down next to each other and waited for the meeting to get under way. I smiled. He smiled.

Man, did I need someone to be smiling at me that day.

I was debating whether Corey would have been freaked out if I told him about Cathy and what I hoped was going to happen to Cathy Marconi's lower intestines when Dave, a guy who had been trying to get voted onto city council for years but had to settle for just being chairman of the alliance, took the stage.

"Okay," he said. "I apologize for the delay. Our special guest for the night had some trouble getting here, but he's arrived, so let's get this show on the road."

Most weeks we have a special guest post-human who comes in to talk about his culture and struggles or whatever. Sometimes they're interesting, and sometimes they're a bore. I've heard enough vampires explaining that they don't really bite people in the neck (at least not anymore) or turn into bats to last me a lifetime.

"Our guest tonight is a member of the species most recently revealed to exist," said Dave, "the group of diminutive post-humans who dwelled in European forests and inspired legends of elves, dwarves, and fairies. Let's give him a hand."

"Oh, this'll be cool," said Corey while we clapped. "I've never met one of those."

"Me neither," I said. "I thought the story was that they were all long dead."

As we clapped, Gregory Grue stepped onto the stage and waddled up to the microphone. He was back in his overcoat and fedora, the ones he'd been wearing that morning.

I almost peed myself when I saw him. The fact that I didn't was probably the best thing that had happened all day.

Then, for a second, I was ashamed to have thought he

was a freak, now that I knew he was some kind of post-human. There are tons of kinds out there besides vampires and zombies, like this group they found out in the Appalachian Mountains. They're almost exactly like normal humans, except that they can turn invisible for a few seconds at a time.

Maybe eating burger wrappers was how Gregory's people got their nutrition or something.

But still—calling me Grimace was *so* not cool, and his people's culture was no excuse, as far as I was concerned.

I lowered myself down in my chair, hoping he wouldn't see me, but trying not to let Corey notice I was freaked out.

"Hoo hoo!" Gregory Grue growled into the microphone. "Sorry I'm late. I was hanging out down at this watering hole on Court Avenue, and then I had to go out to pick up some supplies. Ended up at this bar down by the river where they make a lot of cocktails with Tang. Missed the bus and ended up hitching a ride out here with some guy who works down at the airport. Nice guy. He couldn't stay, but here I am. Gregory Grue! How do you do?"

There was some very polite applause.

"My people don't really care to be called fairies, or elves, or dwarves," Gregory went on. "We prefer the title we took several hundred years ago: the People of Peace. We dwelled in the forests of Ireland for thousands of years, living in harmony with nature, before we were driven out. And tonight, I come before you to stand behind you, and present to you a piece of my people's traditional poetry."

He straightened up as well as he could, paused, then said with great gravity,

"Ladies and gentlemen, take my advice:
pull down yer pants an' slide on the ice!"

He paused for another second, then said, "Because you can't get suspended for taking your butt to school. Thank you very much!"

He bowed, winked in my direction, and hobbled his way off the stage to polite, confused applause while I tried not to start hyperventilating.

"Well, that was pretty awful," Corey said, to my great relief.

"He didn't sound like he was from the forests of Ireland," I said. "More like the taverns of Detroit."

"I'll bet he's not even a real post-human," said Corey. "He's probably one of those fakers who was pretending to be a Vietnam vet before."

"Yeah," I said. "If he's a post-human, then I have purple teeth."

"Oh really?" he asked. "Let me see!"

I showed my teeth, and he reached out and touched one of the front ones.

It was as close as I'd come to kissing anyone in a long time.

And if it wasn't a sign that he liked me, what was?

"Nope. Pearly white," he said.

I smiled, curling my lips up just enough that they brushed his finger as he pulled it away.

It felt good to feel like someone liked me.

"Okay," said Dave, who looked pretty embarrassed as he went back to the microphone. "Thank you, Mr. Grue, for that, uh, enlightening presentation. I knew that poem as a child, but I didn't realize it was of . . . post-human origin."

"Pre-human!" Gregory shouted offstage.

"Okay," said Dave. "Sure. Now, let's get on down to business. It's homecoming season, as you all know."

I slyly nudged Corey's foot with mine.

"So," said Dave, "we're all going to be on alert, since we're hearing all the same rumors about Wilhelm and what's left of his clan that go around every time there's a dance coming up. We've had no reports of attacks or sightings, though, so let's just stay on guard. We will have a contingent of vampires on call, ready to intervene, right?"

"Yeah," Murray called out. "There'll be an honor guard of about a dozen of us stationed around Cornersville Trace High the night of the dance. We're on call starting tonight, just in case."

"Any reason to think any of Wilhelm's clan is coming back for revenge?"

"Nah," said Murray. "But they've all been told to stay out of Iowa, so if they show up, it'll be curtains for those bozos. Pow!"

He made a punching motion and everyone chuckled a bit.

"I'm sure it won't be necessary," said Dave. "But, well, rumors are rumors, and you know how the students there get whenever they have a dance. No offense, Jennifer."

"None taken," I said.

Ever since Alley Rhodes had been attacked at a prom, people got weird when there was a dance coming up—partly because Will's clan had vowed revenge when they got kicked out of town, and partly out of just plain paranoia. Fred was known simply to stay home the whole week around prom to keep from getting harassed.

At the end of the meeting, everyone got up to mingle while Gregory Grue played something that sounded like "Dance of the Sugar-Plum Fairy" on the piano. Most people ignored him. I don't think anyone else believed he was a post-human, either, but we were all too polite to confront him over it.

Corey hadn't said anything about homecoming.

I decided that maybe he was just too shy. Maybe he didn't want to risk freaking me out and screwing up our friendship.

Obviously, I'd have to take matters into my own hands.

I'd sure as hell never asked a guy out before, but I'd had too bad a day to let it end with *more* disappointment.

Damn the torpedos and full speed ahead!

St. Jennifer the Purple for the win!

After all, if I didn't, Amber would be totally disappointed. I didn't want to let her down.

As Corey and I sipped coffee from the urn in the corner of the armory, I made my move.

"Are you going to the homecoming dance at Valley?" I asked.

"Maybe," he said.

"What's stopping you?"

He smiled a little.

Here it comes, I told myself. *He's going to say "Probably, but I'm not sure the girl I like will go with me,"* then he'll tell me that *I'm the girl. . . .*

"It's the same night as the dance at Hoover, and I think Emily wants to go to that one," he said.

Did you ever hear someone say their heart had sunk? That's what happened. I actually felt it drop about five inches from my chest into my stomach. I swear I even felt it bounce off my kidneys.

But I tossed some hair around to look casual.

"Who's Emily?" I asked.

"She's this girl who goes to Hoover," he said.

"Are you guys, like . . . together?" I asked, calmly, and like I wasn't about to freaking die.

"Well, not officially," he said. "But we'll see."

I smiled a little, but I felt like all the color was draining out of my hair, and all the blood was draining out of my heart.

"But hey," he said, "if she doesn't want to go, I might just go to the one at Valley with a group. You could come along, if you want."

"Whatever," I muttered.

Super.

A few minutes later I excused myself and tromped out to my car. *Tromped.*

Freezing rain was coming down again—the kind of icy rain that stings like hell against your cheeks. I was convinced that it was coming down just to spite me.

If it hadn't been so cold and nasty out, I wouldn't have taken skates to school.

If I hadn't done that, I wouldn't have gotten suspended, and Cathy would have had no reason to give me that look of hers. I might not have been so desperate to turn the day around by getting Corey to ask me out. I could have just gone on living a little while longer in the hope that he'd ask *me* out sooner or later.

This day had sucked eggs.

Rotten ones.

Runny rotten ones.

A lousy, crappy, soul-sucking, butt-sniffing, very bad day.

And if Corey didn't like me, where did he even get off going around touching my teeth like that? Not cool.

As much as I hated to admit it, I'd never really had a boyfriend. I'd barely even had time to have a crush on anyone.

And now I was almost eighteen and had barely been kissed. If I let myself think about it too much, I felt like a total loser.

A big purple loser.

I had really thought Corey would break my losing streak.

He had probably just been toying with the idea of dating someone like me so that people would see us together and say, "Wow, he's going out with someone who looks like *that*? He must really be open-minded!"

Dick.

Of course, that was almost exactly what I'd been doing with him. I hadn't really been *that* into him. But now that I knew he didn't want me, I was bummed. If a girl doesn't have a guy's heart to break, she can always just break her own.

As I sat down in my car, I tried not to think about Corey, and ended up thinking about Mutual Scrivener, the boy who should have been my first kiss, instead.

Thinking about Mutual was a bad, bad idea for me.

Yes, Mutual is a real person. I know I've said in interviews that he was a plot device that Eileen made up, but that was just to protect him, really, since he comes off as a real loser in the book, and he's totally not. He is kind of a dork, but he could hardly help it, given the way he was raised.

Lots of normal people homeschool their kids these days, but Mutual's parents weren't among them. They were . . . well, the kind of people who would give a kid a name like Mutual. When they signed him up to attend sixth grade at Gordon Liddy, the old grade school in Preston, I think it was the first time they'd ever let him out of the house. He showed up for his first day in a blazer and dinner plate–sized glasses, and he never used contractions when he spoke, just like the seventeen-year-old version of him in *Born to Be Extraordinary*.

He might have been the biggest dork in history, but I thought he was sort of . . . exotic. It didn't take much to seem exotic in Preston back then, but he fascinated me.

And I found out that he liked me, too. He started reading Shakespeare to impress me—which totally worked. Jason and Amber, who taught him most of the major swear words and introduced him to the joy of heavy metal, worked hard to fix him up with me.

A week after we'd both lost at the district spelling bee, we made an appointment to meet in the woods between the playground and the street the next day to kiss.

But the day we made that plan was the last time I'd ever seen him. He and his parents had vanished the next morning.

I got about one postcard a year from him saying "I'm okay," but they all had different postmarks, so I had no idea where he was. I had tried and failed to find him online about a hundred times. It was a dead-end mystery that just kept giving me glimmers of hope that I'd see him again some-day.

Those glimmers of hope can wreck you, you know. They'll keep you chasing something like it's a dollar on a string in an old silent comedy. Even when you know you should just move on.

Flirting with Corey had helped me a lot, but now that I didn't have him to focus on, I'd probably be going back to drawing pictures of what Mutual might look like now (since pining over an eleven-year-old is just icky) and fantasizing about him showing back up, saving me from my mundane life and showing me how to become the extraordinary ver-sion of myself that I always dreamed of being (and that I wish I'd never told Eileen about).

But all that pining would just end up hurting me. He was gone. I hadn't gotten a postcard from him in over a year now.

Falling back into a crush on him would be a bad way to finish off a lousy day.

And the day hadn't finished sucking yet. Driving home in the sleet was going to be a pain in the neck, and the way my luck was going, I'd slide off the slippery road, the car would flip over, and they'd end up hosing what was left of me into the Raccoon River along with the dirty slush.

I shook my head and tried to file all my misery into its own compartment so I could focus on driving. Then I turned the key in my ignition, and, as I should have guessed, noth-ing happened.

The engine didn't even *try* to start.

Ten minutes went by, and the car still wasn't starting. Not even sputtering, like it usually did when it was stalled.

I was about to pull out my phone and call for a ride when

the dashboard lights turned on and the radio blasted to life, playing ragtime piano music. The engine started to hum, and there was a tap at the window.

"Hoo hoo!"

Gregory Grue was standing next to my car, smoking a cigar.

"Just let me take out my wand and the spell will be cast!" said the fairy godmother. She took out her magic wand and began to wave it in circles over Jenny's head. . . .

five

If you're reading this, I assume you read Eileen's book, so you know that "Just let me take out my wand" is the fairy god-mother's catchphrase. Even if you haven't read the book, I'm sure you've seen "Just Let Me Take Out My Wand" on a T-shirt or something.

If Gregory Grue had tried to say anything like "Just let me take out my wand," I probably would have tried to bash his skull in before he could make another move.

But he didn't, thank God.

He just looked into my window and said, "Mind if we talk for a second?"

I shrugged, and he let himself into the backseat of the car, where he made himself comfortable, stretching out his legs, which weren't long enough to fill the whole backseat.

Up close, I saw that he had a smoker's face; like he wasn't really old, exactly, but he was already wrinkled. He looked like he would have had more teeth than most people, except that he was missing a few.

"Who the hell are you, really?" I asked. "You're obviously not a post-human."

He smiled and tossed a handful of sparkly glitter in the air.

"I'm your fairy godmother!" he announced as the glitter rained down on him. The sound of some trumpets going "Dun duh duh DUN!" blared up on my radio at just the right second, interrupting the ragtime piece.

"Give me a break," I said. "Fairy godmother?"

He laughed, then coughed, then laughed, then coughed some more, then scratched his neck and coughed some more.

"That's as good a title as any. I'm here to make your life all better. But I'm nobody's mommy, so let's just say I'm your fairy godmofo, okay?"

He laughed again.

"You're full of crap," I said.

"You don't have to believe me," he said. "Not yet. You will. And it's *pre*-human, kiddo. We've been around since before you humans started screwing everything up and drove my people out of the forest."

"At least quit smoking in my car, all right?"

He lazily took another drag on the cigar, totally ignoring me, and looked out the window.

"What do they call you bow-necked hawkeyes, anyway? Iowish?"

"Iowan," I said.

"Iowan." He nodded. "I like the word for people who live in Michigan better. Michiganders. Sounds like a bird."

"I guess," I said.

"The name for Minneapolis people is good, too. Min-neapolitan. Sounds tasty."

He exhaled right in my face again, right at my eyes this time. I clenched them shut till the smell died out, but when I opened my eyes the smoke was still curling around me, making weird shapes that I don't think smoke is supposed to make. Like, I could see little miniature faces that were moving their lips in the smoke curls.

Freaky.

"How about people from Des Moines?" he asked. "Demoinic?"

"I don't know," I said. "Will you please just tell me what you want?"

He sat up.

"Every now and then, my people get a little bit of magic to play with," he said, "and I'm using mine to help you out. I can see that you need it."

"I don't need any help," I said. "Not from you."

"I read your file," he said. "And I think I've got you figured out. You thought you had a chance with lover-boy in there, but he turned you down, right?"

"Shut up."

"And you act like the purple hair isn't to get attention, but it secretly is."

"Shut up!"

"You dropped all your extra activities, but you fritter away all the time you saved. And you tell yourself that most of your problems are because of Cathy or Mrs. Smollet or your parents, but the truth is you know you're just . . . not . . . good enough."

He flashed me his goblin grin. Like the Cheshire cat's,

his grin was exactly the shape of a crescent moon and made me feel like he knew things I didn't want him to.

Like that he was absolutely right.

I worried every day that I wasn't *really* an interesting, free-spirited, extraordinary girl, and the purple hair was just a lame attempt to look like one. That the real me was going to turn out to be a total bore. Or, worse, a violent lunatic.

I mean, I got along well with people. My teachers all liked me—I even had coffee with my old sixth-grade teacher now and then.

But nobody except Jason and Amber really knew about my dark side. The side that spent a lot of time fantasizing about murdering people and dancing on their graves.

Gregory took another puff of his cigar.

"Not to mention you pretend you don't want a part in the big show."

"I don't," I said. "Being onstage gives me spelling bee flashbacks."

He chuckled. "It says in your school file that you were quite the little speller once upon a time," he said. "You don't miss anything about those days? No one who used to compete with you?"

I thought of Mutual Scrivener, the boy I had liked and who liked me back. He had been signed up for public school *just* to be in the spelling bees, and disappeared shortly after the last one. He was a guy from those days, all right. And I did miss him.

But I said, "No. Nothing. I hated being in those things. They used to make *way* too big a deal of them in Preston."

"Now, look, kiddo," Gregory said. "I think you've got a

lot of potential. You really do. A few good wishes ought to help you out, and I'm prepared to grant you three reasonable ones, as long as you get a guy of my choice to kiss you during the homecoming dance."

"If you say that *you're* the guy of your choice, I'll kick you in the crotch," I said.

He just laughed. "Relax, girly girl. I'm a teacher. That would be highly inappropriate. It won't be me at all. No one you'd totally hate to kiss, as long as you keep an open mind."

"Who's the guy?"

"You'll find out soon," he said.

"I don't think I'm going to take this deal," I said. "Three wishes I don't believe you'd grant in exchange for a favor you won't even tell me all the details of? Screw it."

"That shows brains, judgment, and maturity," he said. "Except that you don't get a choice. The spell is cast, the tale is told. Et cetera."

"That's not fair!" I said.

"That's the way the coffee drips," he told me. "I don't make the rules here, I just follow them. But at least you get some wishes out of the deal."

"I don't want anything from you," I said. "Why should I even believe that you're for real?"

He chuckled and took another drag on his cigar. "We don't carry credentials, but I'm in the giving vein today, so I'll prove it if you want. What are you going to do, ask me to make a unicorn appear?"

"Yes," I said. "That'll do. Get me a unicorn. I want one in my backyard."

In fairy tales, if you ask a fairy for something impossible, they usually end up tearing themselves to pieces or something. But Gregory Grue smirked.

"Early humans tried to exterminate unicorns, you know," he said. "Best thing humans ever did."

"You think driving an animal to extinction is good?" I asked.

"I do when their crap smells as bad as unicorn crap. You've never smelled anything as bad as unicorn crap, honey. Not even if you've been in the men's room of the bus stop in Passaic, New Jersey. Wouldn't you rather I just made your car smell like that? The cleanup would be easier."

"You just can't get a unicorn," I said. "You're probably planning to fart and say you made the smell appear magically."

"Look," he said, "I can't get you a unicorn out of thin air. I *can* get you one, and I won't even count it as a wish, but it'll take a day or two. When it gets here, you'll know I'm serious beyond any doubt."

"Fair enough," I said. "Get me a unicorn and I'll never doubt you again."

"Okay," he said. "You can slack off and not believe me until then, if you want. But either way, I owe you three wishes, so close your eyes and think of the bestest wishes you can, kiddo."

He blew some more smoke at me, and I closed my eyes— not so much because he told me to as to keep from getting smoke in them.

"Now, wish!" he said.

So I wished.

"I wish you would go away," I said.

"I will once you've made a few good wishes for me to pick from," he said. "So get at it."

The smoke started to cloud my brain—I still don't know what was in that cigar. But I started talking.

"I wish I had a million dollars."

"Be less obvious, please. And more realistic. Let me help you out. What do you *really* wish for, in those parts of your brain you hoped the purple dye would seep into and cover up?"

He blew even more smoke and I felt it swirling around in my nostrils. I felt myself go light-headed, and started saying things without even thinking about them.

"I wish I could get revenge on Cathy."

"Swell. What else?"

"I wish Emily would tell Corey to go to hell."

"That's harsh, kiddo, but consider it done. Anything else?"

I paused.

"I wish I could find an old friend who moved away."

"Nice," he said. "Now think of the rest of your wishes. Wish for the things you won't say out loud. Like being in the play."

Everything went silent for a few seconds. When I opened my eyes, the smoke was gone and Gregory was still smiling, so wide that I was pretty sure he'd be sore in the morning. And I felt like I'd just come up for air after being underwater.

He threw some more glitter over his head and blew another puff of smoke. This one was so big that it filled up my entire car. Through the smoke, I heard him say, "Your wishes are granted. Long live Gregory Grue!"

I was afraid for a second that I was about to suffocate in the fumes, but they started to dissipate.

I was aware of the music stopping and the engine ceasing to purr, and when the smoke was gone, Gregory, the raggedy "fairy godmofo," was gone, too.

There was no lingering smell from the cigar.

There was no glitter left in the seats, either.

The only tangible sign left that anyone had been there was a swear word written in the frost on the outside of the rear window.

As the fairy godmother flew away, Jenny felt as though she had been changed already.

Amber came back to the car, holding the two diet sodas. "Are you okay?" she asked concernedly. "You look different!"

"I'm fine," said Jenny. "Just fine."

But she was different, all right.

She would never be the same.

six

I sat in my car in silence for a second, shivering from the cold, trying to process everything, and wondering if I should go ask someone back in the armory for help.

Gregory, I decided, must be one of those substitute teachers you see on TV and in movies now and then who come out of nowhere and really inspire kids before moving on. Or anyway, that's what he was *trying* to do. Normally those guys pick some disadvantaged kid who never had a chance, but since Cornersville Trace is pretty damned middle class, he just pinpointed the chubby girl who apparently had a discipline problem as the most pathetic person in school—the one who needed his help the most.

And he thought I was dumb enough that a bunch of magic tricks would make me believe he was a "fairy godmother" so he could inspire me to reach my full potential. He'd give me a part in the show or something and say he'd granted my wish, giving me a whole buttload of newfound self-esteem.

Nice try, Gregory Grue.

This all made me feel super.

If he were really magic, he would have gotten me the million dollars.

I still didn't understand why there was no glitter left in the seats, but I assumed he'd used some cheap "disappearing glitter" trick he bought from a magic shop or something.

I decided that I should just head home, but when I turned the key, the car had gone back to being stalled. Whatever Gregory had done to make it seem like it was working again must have been a trick, too.

After fifteen minutes of turning the key, I was freezing my butt off and the car still wasn't starting. Jason was at work and Amber didn't have her license, so I went back and forth for a few minutes deciding which parent to call. On the one hand, I didn't really want to deal with my dad. On the other, he might be able to fix the car, so I wouldn't have to pay for a tow truck.

I wasn't exactly flush with cash—no thanks to Gregory and his inability to get me a million bucks.

Eventually, I just called Dad and prepared for a lecture.

When he showed up half an hour later and walked over to the car, he stared at the cussword on the window.

"Rough neighborhood," he said.

"Kids," I said. "One minute they're buckling their knickerbockers below the knee and hiding dime novels in the corncrib, and the next thing you know they're writing the S-word on car windows. Makes your blood boil, well I should say!"

"Can we go one evening without you talking like you're a character in *The Music Man*, please?" he asked.

"No promises," I said.

He tinkered under the hood for a second, then asked me to start her up. I turned the key, and there were sparks, but the engine still didn't start.

"Sorry, Jen," he said. "I'll call and have it towed some-place tomorrow morning."

Super.

I climbed out of my car and into Dad's. He started it up and we cruised out of the parking lot and into the streets of Des Moines.

"Your mom called the admissions people at Drake," he said. "They said the suspension won't be an issue, as long as it's a one-time thing."

"Well, that's a relief," I said.

"I don't know how you think you're going to get through college, though," he said. "The kind of workload you've given yourself this year won't prepare you for it."

"Dad," I said, "I just had a crappy day followed by a crappy night, and I have this weird feeling that I'm having a nervous breakdown. Can we hold off on the lecture?"

He sighed and backed down, but the worst of it was that he sort of had a point. I was slacking off, big-time, and not really feeling any closer to being the person I wanted to be-come than I had been before.

We drove through the freezing rain and Dad seemed to know enough not to try to make me feel any worse. I don't like throwing pity parties for myself, but I thought I'd earned one for the evening.

I did feel different, though. Like the Jenny in the book.

I'd driven through the suburbs of Des Moines, down Eighty-Sixth Street, a million times. Nothing had changed. But for some reason, everything suddenly seemed a tiny bit different on that trip. It almost felt like I'd traveled forward in time, but not very far. Like, three years or something. Everything seemed the same, but different.

Just like my whole life. Different, but not different enough to matter too much.

It was a weird feeling.

When Dad dropped me off, he stared up at the Wells Fargo Wagon in the driveway.

"Was there anything good inside it?" he asked.

"Not that I know of," I told him.

"It looks loaded," he said. "You might want to check."

I assumed he had hidden something there, like an envelope full of brochures for the MBA program at Drake. I *thought* he'd given up on that when my sister, Val, got out of an expensive business school and found out that a master's degree and a 4.1 GPA don't really qualify you for any more jobs than an undergrad degree in art history does these days, but you never can tell with Dad.

I made a point of walking right past the wagon, then made sure there was no unicorn in the backyard. There wasn't.

But after Dad had driven away, I went to see if my Wells Fargo Wagon had, in fact, come stocked with rocking chairs, double boilers, and all the other stuff the people of River City, Iowa, had ordered in the show.

All I saw at first was a bunch of empty cardboard boxes.

However, taped to one of the boxes was a postcard addressed to me.

Dear Jennifer,

I'm still okay. Hope to see you soon.

Mutual

I sat there and read it over and over, even though it was just eight words.

It couldn't be real.

There was no postmark. And no reason in the world that there should be a postcard on the wagon for me from *anyone*. Gregory must have read my file and found that newspaper article about the spelling bee—the one that described Mutual as my boyfriend (which was totally embarrassing at the time). This was simply part of his attempt to trick me into thinking he was magic.

But it looked like Mutual's handwriting to me.

And how would Gregory have known that I tended to get postcards from Mutual in mysterious ways, as if he had no way of actually mailing them and had to find sneaky ways to send them to me?

Like, one time a guy just knocked on the door and said he found the postcard in a truck full of pumpkins and felt like he should drop it off.

Maybe Gregory was for real after all.

And really was granting my wish.

If Mutual was the guy he wanted me to kiss at the dance,

and he was willing to magically help make it possible, I would never say another word against him, even if he was a creep.

I took the postcard indoors and went to my room to look up the news story about fairies being real. On the off chance that you haven't already found this out, just typing "fairies" into a search engine isn't really going to get you much information—mostly just a bunch of pictures of Tinker Bell and stuff. Probably pictures of me now, too. Nothing about "real" ones, except for those pictures that a couple of English girls took a hundred years ago, which look totally fake to me.

Eventually I dug up some news stories where some of the older vampires said there was some group of short posthumans that had lived in the woods years ago, but no one knew much about them, except that they were all long dead. An archaeologist backed the story up with pottery fragments she'd found, but no one really knew what this group could do, exactly. Whatever powers or abilities they had had obviously hadn't been enough to keep them from being driven from the forests.

There was no mention of magic. No one knew anything about magic being real—all the stuff vampires could do was because of protein mutations, not magic. If the guys in the forests could turn invisible or anything, that was probably just a bodily function the rest of us didn't have.

The next day, I called Murray and asked if he knew much about fairies. He just groaned.

"Look," he said, "we don't know about every post-human group in the world. Every now and then you hear about some weird tribe that lives inside the hills and comes out for one month every hundred years to play nine-pins or something, but as far as I know, it's all BS, and those guys who got driven out of the forests are all dead."

"So, you weren't buying that guy last night, either?"

He laughed. "That was just some putz who wanted the twenty-buck honorarium Dave pays to speakers," he said. "Probably an out-of-work actor."

"He's working for the drama department at my school," I said.

"See? Actor."

"Why would Dave even book him?" I asked.

"Well, Dave probably didn't believe him, either," said Murray. "But he's got a tough job trying to find a post-human every week in Des Moines. He's sort of running out of options by now. You remember that werewolf two weeks ago?"

"Sure."

"Fake. That was just a hairy guy. Like Robin Williams. Personally, I think more vampires should move to Des Moines, because all these insurance-industry jobs here are perfect for dead people, but that whole thing with Wilhelm three years ago scares 'em away."

So that was that. Gregory was no post-human, according to someone who'd been living as one since the seventeen hundreds. He was just some weird actor/substitute teacher trying to motivate me or something.

All he knew about Mutual would have come from whatever file they had on me at the office—the file was probably full of newspaper articles about the bee. But maybe there had been a postcard for me from Mutual in the file that had been sent to the school for some reason.

I figured that I had solved the mystery already.

That night in bed, I tried to force myself into a crush on a movie star or something. It was no use falling back into a crush on a boy I would probably never see again.

You know where you stand with movie stars, at least. You can't really get hurt.

But that night, I had vivid, extremely naughty dreams.

About Fred the vampire.

Cathy's boyfriend.

Every girl wished she could date Fred, the vampire prince. His royal tattoo made them swoon. But only Jenny, who had caught him reading Chaucer when it wasn't even assigned, knew that he had the soul of a poet.

She wished she could stare at his tattoo all day.

seven

The Fred in the book was actually based on Jason, not the real Fred. You'll notice Eileen never says what part of Fred the "royal tattoo" was on.

Jason was hoping to freak Eileen out when he pulled down his pants to show her his tattoo during her interview with us, but, well, she swooned when she saw his butt.

She's a butt swooner. That's what she is. A cheese-sucking butt swooner.

"That," she told me later, "is the kind of boy girls want! Not the real Fred. So I'm going to have Fred act more like Jason."

Now that most of the vampires have been banned from high schools, people sort of forget that most vampire students were total losers. Seriously—you know how at every school there's one guy in his twenties who still hangs around by the football field all the time? Imagine how much bigger a loser that guy would have to be to keep hanging around when he was two hundred. At least Fred was only about fifty or sixty.

The real Fred looked okay, but he wasn't "hot." He had kind of a ratty look, with one of those scraggly teenage mustaches, and acne that had lasted for decades (poor guy). He wasn't the prince of anything. And he wasn't exactly a rebel—the guy had stayed in high school *way* longer than he really needed to. How rebellious could he be?

I tried to explain this to Eileen, but she just laughed.

"Girls don't want to read that he wasn't that great a catch," she said. "They want the main character to be just like them, and they want the love interest to be the exact kind of guy they want to date, and they want them to live happily ever after."

"You're just pandering to them," I said.

"And they'll love it!" she said. "Everyone needs wish fulfillment!"

Fair enough. Wish fulfillment is as good a reason to read a book as any, I guess. I read books for that, too, sometimes.

But I'm not trying to make you be my best friend or make you think I'm just like you with this book. I don't want you thinking you need to be a princess or have a fairy godmother to become extraordinary, either. I'm hoping you'll figure out that you have to become extraordinary on your own terms, not wait for some guy to *make* you that way, even though it might be hard work. I am trying to forge in the smithy of my soul the uncreated conscience of our generation, or something like that.

In other words, I'm here to tell the truth. And, as hard as it's been for me to admit, sometimes the truth was that I was just as likely to turn into a terrible, violent, spiteful person as I was to turn into a peace-loving, intellectual hippie chick who acted like one of those crazy English teachers in sitcoms or one of those eccentric women in screwball comedies. I could have been extraordinarily *mean*.

Beyond that, the truth is that I didn't like Fred much at all. I thought he was a real dick, and never really stopped to think about *why* he became a dick, or to consider that anyone who had spent thirty or forty years unable to get his skin to clear up was liable to be pretty bitter. Just try to calculate how many zits you'd have to pop if you had a forty-year case of acne. When you're done barfing, you'll have some idea of why most teenage vampires seem so depressed.

So I had never liked him much, and wasn't at *all* jealous of Cathy, but I woke up Monday morning feeling like I had a crush on him. You know, like you do whenever you have a dream about someone. Especially one of *those* kinds of dreams.

And all I could think of was how much it would suck for Cathy if *I* were the one he took to the dance.

In fact, as I got ready for school, I sort of fell in love with the idea. I imagined a group forming around Fred and me as we spun in the center of the dance floor, while Cathy cried and threw a tantrum in the corner.

And then the band would start a fast number, everyone would start dancing, and she'd be trampled to a messy death.

Yeah.

Man, that sounded good.

Still want your daughters on my lawn, moms?

Sure, it's cute when Junie B. Jones fantasizes about people

she doesn't like getting "stompled" to death by ponies, but I know it wasn't my most attractive habit.

Anyway, I nursed the crush on Fred all morning, careful not to let it get so serious that it would hurt to see him with Cathy, but letting it stay strong enough that it would keep me from falling back into a crush on Mutual until something better came along.

When it came time for the rehearsal in fourth period, I walked in and saw Gregory Grue deep in conversation with Eileen Codlin in the back row of the auditorium.

"Now, Richard the Third, the real one, was actually my favorite king," he was saying. "He wasn't nearly as bad as Shakespeare made him look. Man, I miss the days when kings would lead soldiers into battle!"

When he saw me standing there, he grinned up at me.

"Jennifer! I believe you know Miss Codlin," Gregory said to me. "She's interviewing me about my experiences as a pre-human for a book."

Eileen turned around and beamed at me.

I rolled my eyes at her. "Do you believe this guy?" I asked.

"I know!" said Eileen, who sort of misread me (a real habit of hers). "One of the last few People of Peace in the world, and he's right here in Iowa! He told me all about how he's helping make your wishes come true, just like a regular fairy godmother."

"Fairy god*mofo*," said Gregory. "Let's call it that. I'm nobody's mother."

She laughed again.

"By the way, Jennifer," he went on, "the school doesn't want to cover the expense of towing the Wells Fargo Wagon from your house, so you'll have to find a way to move it."

"I'm not paying for it," I said.

"Then you'll have to be creative," he said.

Eileen probably thought *that* was him trying to inspire and challenge me, too.

I rolled my eyes and took a seat behind Cathy, where she wouldn't see me. I wasn't up to looking her in the eye, and if I confronted her she'd just say I was planning to attack her again.

She was holding court among a bunch of freshmen. She was doing her first show—and it had totally gone to her head.

"I want to do a really serious, *difficult* role next time," she was saying. "Like, I want to see a parent die. Or have to breast-feed onstage. They can do that at some colleges."

I giggled as quietly as I could as she went on about how she was going to stay awake for seventy-two hours to look old and frumpy enough for her role as the mayor's wife. That was okay for opening night, but I hated to think what she'd look like for the Saturday show.

Wouldn't it have been easier just to *act*?

One time at the Shakespeare Club (which I still attended, since it wasn't a school club), we had this speaker who said the reason Shakespeare was so brilliant was that he was more alive than everyone else. Like, the average person walking down the street was maybe 50 percent alive, but Shakespeare was 100 percent alive. He saw layers of meaning in every mundane thing that happened. He could, like, hear the secrets of the universe blowing in the wind.

I didn't feel like I could be much more than 20 percent alive myself. But at least I didn't think that getting a small role in a high school play made me the toast of the New York avant-garde or whatever.

Once she noticed I was behind her, Cathy turned to me.

"Hi," she said.

I just stared at her.

"Hey," she said. "I'm totally sorry about yesterday."

"Yeah, right," I said.

"Seriously," she said. "I thought they'd just, like, scare you a little. I didn't know they'd toss you into suspension!"

She snickered, like it was funny or something. It wasn't funny to me.

I was about to tell her so when the bell rang and Gregory Grue jumped up onto the stage.

"Hoo hoo!" he shouted. "Another rehearsal is upon us, and another chance to improve the show, yourselves, and your community. As your director, I'm going to be making some changes in the casting toward all those ends. Where's Cathy Marconi?"

Cathy raised her hand.

"You're the mayor's wife? Eulalie Shinn?"

"Yes," she said.

"Not anymore," he said. "You're in the chorus from now on."

"*What?*" Cathy shouted.

Then she went into a bit of a rant. This is one of the parts of the story where I'm cleaning up the language.

Gregory just nodded and ignored her.

"Jennifer Van Den Berg," he said, "can you come up onstage, please?"

I wandered up and stepped onstage, feeling like everyone was staring at me, which I wasn't really used to back then.

"You're the mayor's wife now, kiddo," he said.

My head started to spin.

Cathy had not sat down yet. She started yelling something about how they didn't have purple-haired women in Iowa in 1912.

"They have wigs for that," Gregory said with a wave of his hand. "And Mrs. Shinn wears hats with brims and feathers that go from here to who laid the rails, so no one'll notice the hair anyway."

Cathy looked like she'd just been smacked in the face with a baseball bat.

And I kind of felt that way myself.

"I'm not an actress," I said to him, quietly.

"Sure you are, kiddo," he said. "I'm pulling you out of the chorus and into the spotlight!"

"I never wished for that!" I said.

He just winked.

Obviously, Gregory couldn't read my mind. He assumed that I wanted to be a star or something, and that getting to sing "Pick-a-Little, Talk-a-Little" would fulfill my destiny.

As I stood on the stage, I started to have spelling bee flashbacks, just like I'd predicted.

When I was a kid, Preston was a very different town. It still had much more of a small-town vibe—the kind of town that probably would have revolved around the high school football team, except that we didn't have a high school at all. The only real local competition we had in town was the spelling bee—and people took it very, very seriously.

In the run-up to the all-school bee, we'd have gamblers hanging around the playground, trying to figure out who to bet on. And then the five kids who went to districts every year were treated like heroes around town—until they lost, when they were treated like dirt. It was more pressure than an eleven-year-old should have to deal with.

And it all came rushing back when I stood onstage. This was *not* the way to help me build my confidence. In fact, I nearly had a panic attack.

"Let's hear it for Jennifer!" said Gregory.

There was one person applauding: Eileen.

Gregory handed me a script and told me to get to work. I spent the rest of the class huddled over in a chair, pretending to be learning my lines while I breathed as deeply as I could and avoided looking in Cathy's direction.

Jason and Amber were giving me a ride home that day, since my car was still in the shop. After school, I met up with them at the back door, where Smollet brought them out from their last day of in-school, and told them how the new director had given me Cathy's part.

Jason laughed. "You getting revenge on her?" he asked.

"I was as surprised as she was," I said. "But I'm still thinking of getting revenge for yesterday. I actually woke up thinking about how awesome it would be if I stole Fred from Cathy."

Amber turned toward me. "You like Fred?" she asked.

"Not *really*," I said. "But I had a dream about him last night, and, well, you know how it is."

I wasn't sure if they *did* know. They had been a couple since, like, before either of them had probably even started puberty. Maybe they'd never had a dream about anyone else.

How awesome is that?

"So now I have a plan," I said. "I'm going to seduce Fred and rub it in Cathy's face."

"Jennifer," Amber said, "I totally believe that you can do any damned thing you feel like."

"So are you in? Can I put you down for casting me a love spell or something?"

She shrugged. "I haven't tried any of that stuff in a while."

When we were kids, Amber was really into the occult. She'd cast circles of protection around her desk on test days and curse people she didn't like. But after the post-human thing, *every* girl was into Wicca and stuff, which a lot of them thought was, like, the next best thing to becoming a vampire. She kind of drifted away from it then.

"We've hung out with Fred a few times at, like, heavy metal vomit parties and stuff," said Jason. "He actually got converted backstage at an Alice Cooper concert in the seventies."

"I heard it was an Ozzy Osbourne concert," I said.

"Nope. Cooper," said Jason. "Ozzy wasn't even a solo act back then, he was still with Black Sabbath. Anyway, Fred was so drugged up at the time that he isn't even sure who did it."

"Ouch," I said.

We drove up Eighty-Second Street, which a few years before had been nothing but cornfields when you got north of Cedar Avenue. Now it was all strip malls and subdivisions full of white houses on streets named after trees. The year before, the last of the corn separating Preston from Cornersville Trace had been plowed up and the land had been developed.

The population had ballooned in the past five years, but half of the original residents had moved out to other, smaller towns. Finding a native Prestonian in Preston was rare now, which was fine with me. None of the people who had put For Sale signs in my yard when I lost the district spelling bee, or accused Mutual of being a traitor, still lived nearby.

There was nothing about the old Preston that I missed.

Except for Mutual, of course.

But I pushed that out of my mind and tried to imagine how Fred looked with his shirt off.

To celebrate finding out she was a fairy, Jenny decided that she should have *more* purple things—starting with her car. She took the car (and her credit card!) to the nearest custom paint shop and had it painted a beautiful metallic purple. . . .

eight

I still don't have a freaking credit card in real life.

And ever since Eileen's stupid book came out, every spare cent I've been able to scrape up has gone to security, legal bills, and all that crap. And it wasn't like I was swimming in money to start with. I owed my mom a pile for car repairs and stuff—by the time of this story, I was already so far behind that I'd have to teach piano lessons clear till Melinda was in high school.

After the Jenmobile broke down at the armory, Dad had it towed to a garage over on Fourteenth. They called the house and said it would be ready during the day on Monday, so Mom drove me out there after she got off work.

She went inside to pay while I sat in her car. This was going to be another chunk of money I owed her. I wasn't even sure I could afford to keep dying my hair purple, let alone have my car painted purple (which I totally would have done if I had the cash—at least I have *that* in common with the "Jenny" in the book).

And when Mom came stomping out of the garage, she looked furious.

"Eight hundred dollars!" she said. "They charged eight hundred dollars!"

"That's more than three times what I paid for the car!" I said.

"Your dad authorized them to do whatever they needed to," she said. "So now we owe Visa another eight hundred bucks."

"Shoot," I said. "If he authorized it, he'd better be planning to help."

She tossed me my keys with a sigh.

"Jennifer, I'm afraid you might have to get used to the idea of living at home next year. For the first semester, at least," she said.

"But I'm already signed up for the dorms!"

"It's a twenty-minute commute from our house to Drake," she said. "It doesn't make sense for us to waste money on a dorm. Not when we're still paying more on Val's student loans than we are on our mortgage."

"We can scrape together the money," I said. "I'm sure we can."

"I wouldn't count on it," said Mom.

I took my keys and stomped back out toward my own car.

"Jen, calm down," Mom called out. "It's not the end of the world."

I didn't listen to her. I just kept walking until I got into my car, and drove off without a damned word.

I realized that paying for a dorm when I only lived five or ten miles away from campus wasn't exactly frugal, but being on my own felt like it was a huge, totally necessary step in separating myself from my old, boring life. I felt like as long as I lived at home, surrounded by Val's old trophies and all the reminders of my old eighty-hour schedule, and with one parent constantly around to nag me and another who still had keys, I'd be stuck as the same old person, no matter what I did with my hair.

As I drove along, I imagined Val's student-loan officer standing in front of my car several times. I was so mad that I wasn't even paying much attention to the road or the speedometer.

Not until I saw the flashing blue lights in my rearview mirror.

I pulled over and a police car pulled up behind me. I shouted a few words (none of which was "shoot" or "darn") at the roof of the car as the cop walked over, then forced myself to be calm as I rolled the window down.

"Something wrong, Officer?" I asked, which I think is standard protocol when you get pulled over.

"I clocked you at fifty-one," he said. "And this is a thirty-five-mile-per-hour road."

"No one goes thirty-five on this road," I said. "Other cars would think I was a bridge or something."

"That's no excuse," he said. "Did you know that you also ran a stop sign back there?"

I shook my head.

"And with ice on the road, too," he said.

I started to cry, but it didn't make him feel bad enough to

let me off with a warning. He gave me a ticket for speeding and failure to stop.

"How much is this going to cost me?" I asked.

"I'd say about four hundred," he said. "And you'll have to go to traffic school. And your insurance will probably go up."

"Great," I said, sniffling.

And he handed me the ticket and read me some legal-speak gobbledygook that I didn't pay any attention to.

"I'd say to have a good day," he said when he was finished, "but . . . well, have a *better* day."

He walked back to his patrol car, and I stayed pulled over until he was out of sight. Once he was gone, I looked up at the roof of my car and screamed at the top of my lungs.

Then I drove exactly one block before my car stalled out again.

It started right back up, but still.

Ugh!

After paying eight hundred bucks, I think I had a right to expect that it would at least get me home without stalling.

Why wouldn't the world just follow my damned instructions?

All the anger and rejection and everything else inside me sort of merged into one big ball of ugly hatred. I couldn't compartmentalize it any longer—the compartments were full.

This called for drastic action.

When I got home, I ran upstairs, reached under the bed, and pulled out my Big Box of Breakables.

I had countless pieces of dollar-store crap in reserve. There is no shortage of tacky, breakable crap at thrift stores and the dollar store.

There were about a dozen porcelain angels in the box. There was a ceramic hand on a little stand with a sign that said "Please Stop the Violence." A whole bunch of cute porcelain kids with really big eyes wearing pajamas with drop-down seats. A tiny ceramic mushroom house that looked like a penis with windows.

There were Santa Claus figurines. Snowman napkin holders. All kinds of tacky Christmas junk.

There were a couple of ceramic toilets that you were supposed to hang on the bathroom door, one of which had a ceramic old guy with a mustache sitting on it and holding his nose.

This was all going to have to go.

I took the box out to the driveway and laid the contents on the sidewalk, then headed back in to get my headphones. This scene called for music.

I spun around to the *Music Man* folder on my phone and cued up "Seventy-Six Trombones," the big, bombastic march.

Then I went back out to the toolshed to find some actual tools—I wanted something more than just a hammer. A bigger, more powerful weapon that took two hands to use. I wished my dad were the kind of dad who owned a sledgehammer, but there wasn't one of those. And most of his tools had gone with him when he moved out.

There was a crowbar, though.

I took it out to the sidewalk, stood before the junk, and raised the crowbar high above my head with one hand while I hit the Play button on my phone with the other. I turned the volume up so high it hurt my ears.

I stood there rethinking the events of the last few days

during the prologue, from Gregory Grue calling me Grimace at McDonald's to getting a traffic ticket right after being told that I probably wouldn't be able to move out for college.

I just let the anger flow through me.

This was not the teenage life that movies, TV shows, and books had promised me (or the one that *Born to Be Extraordinary* is promising you). I had been cheated.

And the dollar-store junk was going to pay.

I lifted the crowbar above my head with both hands and felt the freezing metal against my fingers. It was so cold that it stung.

The wind picked up, howling through the trees and into my face. It was almost as if I were controlling the weather.

The prologue ended, the brass band kicked in, and "Seventy-Six Trombones" began. I brought the sledge-hammer down on its first victim with a roar just as Harold Hill sang the word "six."

The little porcelain angel crumbled under the weight of my mighty crowbar, and I brought it down on him again a few times, all to the rhythm of the music.

Then I showed a ceramic Santa Claus who was boss.

Seventy-six trombones hit the counterpoint, and the crowbar hit a miniature clown whose pants were falling down.

Then, just to mix things up, I swung the crowbar like a golf club into the ceramic mushroom house that looked like a penis, sending it rolling across the lawn in two or three pieces. I ran after the biggest chunk and brought the crowbar down again and again on the most thingy-like part, screaming all the while.

When there was nothing of the mushroom house left, I stomped back to the sidewalk, where the rest of the stuff was waiting for me.

Boom! The crowbar hit a ceramic Easter bunny with buckteeth.

Crash! Another dollar-store angel bit the pavement.

Clunk! The crowbar hit the damp sidewalk beneath the bits of rubble.

It was almost like dancing, especially as long as I swung the crowbar to the rhythm of the song.

Soon all that was left on the square of sidewalk was dust. The song faded out and turned into the next song on the sound track, a barbershop quartet song about love.

I ignored the music and shouted at the sky.

"When you come to a lawn where the angels lie dead and not a weenie-shaped house is standing, you will know that I have been here. And you will know that I am the Dark Lord Jennifer the Purple! And you will be afraid!"

It probably looked funny to anyone who might have been watching, but I was completely serious at the time. I screamed again as I brought the crowbar down a couple more times on what was left of the big-eyed kids in pajamas.

Yeah. I was kind of off the deep end. I know.

But destroying twenty bucks' worth of tacky crap was something I could afford. Actual therapy was not.

I was so wrapped up in my little reign of terror, and the music, that I didn't notice a car pulling into my driveway, next to the Wells Fargo Wagon.

Then I heard a voice behind me.

"Jennifer?"

I turned around and saw Jason's car. The door opened, and Jason, Amber, and another guy stepped out.

"Look who we found!" said Amber.

The third person was a pale, muscular guy wearing a flannel shirt over a heavy metal T-shirt. His hair hung to his shoulders, with bangs that nearly reached his glasses.

For a second, I didn't recognize him. I stood there and stared while the barbershop quartet sang on in the headphones that hung over my shoulder.

But then he smiled.

"Oh my God," I said.

Mutual Scrivener was standing in front of the Wells Fargo Wagon.

What is love? 'tis not hereafter;
Present mirth hath present laughter;
What's to come is still unsure:
In delay there lies no plenty;
Then come kiss me, sweet and twenty,
Youth's a stuff will not endure.

—Shakespeare (Eat your heart out, Codlin!)

nine

Now, look, people—I know I'm not exactly F. Scott Fitzgerald or anything. I keep trying to work more dazzling imagery into this book besides all the stuff about cold, wet leaves, but it's not easy. I keep waking up from nightmares about reviewers saying I don't use enough "strong verbs" or use too many adverbs or whatever.

So I don't want to dwell too much on how bad a writer Eileen is. At least I have an excuse for my own writing: I'm a sophomore in college right now, and I've never really done any creative writing before. You can't devise standardized tests for creative writing, so we never did it in school.

Eileen practiced writing for years to develop her clumsy, inelegant third-person voice, her awkward mixed metaphors, and her convoluted sentences.

But again, I don't want to rant about her—I just want to point out how the real story went differently than the story in the book.

Mutual really did come back into my life the same week I met my fairy godmother, just like in *Born to Be Extraordinary*.

In the book, "Jenny" and Mutual are childhood sweethearts, which is at least partly true. And she nursed a crush on him after he moved away, like I did. But when the "book Mutual" was younger, he was a cool, athletic kid with a jet-powered bike and a designer backpack.

And when he sweeps back into her life all of a sudden, he's become a total nerd who wears a blazer and dinner-plate glasses and never uses contractions when he talks.

It was sort of the opposite in real life—he really did wear the blazer and talk sort of like a robot or serial killer or something when we were kids. It was a side effect of being raised by his old-fashioned, agoraphobic, weirdo parents.

Now, as he stood in my driveway, six years since I'd last seen him, his hair was longer, his glasses smaller. And the boy was *ripped*. His muscles were practically breaking through the Metallica T-shirt he was wearing, which I think was Jason's. Jason is a wiry little guy. Next to him, Mutual looked like a bodybuilder.

In Eileen's book, Mutual is always running up to Jenny and trying to kiss her. And if he can do it before she kisses Fred at the dance, it will break the spell, and the princess-ship will go to someone else, for some reason.

In all my fantasies of finding Mutual again, I had imagined him running up and giving me that kiss we'd planned on years earlier. Maybe he'd even say those lines from Shakespeare I just quoted, which basically mean "we won't be young forever, so let's not waste our time."

But he didn't run up to me, like he did in my fantasies or in Eileen's book.

He just stood there. He was smiling, but he looked scared.

I couldn't do anything but stare, either.

I dropped the crowbar, took a step closer to him, and got a good look.

He was older now, naturally—it stands to reason that everyone who's not a vampire will look older at seventeen or eighteen than they did when they were eleven.

"Oh my God," I said. "It's you!"

"Hi," he said, softly. "Remember me?"

"Of course," I said. "I got your postcards."

"All of them?" he asked.

"How many did you send?"

"About a hundred and fifty," he muttered. He was blushing a little. I could see it in the fading light.

Oh my God. He had sent me a hundred and fifty postcards.

The wind blew and sent a bunch of brown leaves flying off the trees toward us. One of them stuck to Mutual's face, but he didn't try to brush it off.

"Then I only got about five percent of them," I said. "I got about one a year. One was in that Wells Fargo Wagon."

"He's been in Alaska this whole time," said Amber. "His parents moved to a farm outside of Anchorage!"

He and I stepped a bit closer to each other.

"There were no stamps or phones or computers in the house," he said, his voice trembling a bit. "I would slip postcards for you into the vegetable crates we shipped out and hope someone would find them and mail them somewhere along the line."

That solved that mystery.

I couldn't control myself any longer—I ran the last couple of steps up to him and hugged him.

I could feel his muscles, but it seemed like he was barely able to stand upright. He barely hugged me back. It was almost like I was holding him up.

"He was on my porch when I got home," said Jason. "My mom said he showed up in a taxi and waited there all day."

"Are your parents back, too?" I asked Mutual.

"No," he said. "If I were two weeks younger, I would be a runaway. I had been wanting to get out, and then this FedEx guy came up to my door with a package for me, and it was a ticket to Des Moines in a purple envelope. I thought one of you had sent it."

"We could never figure out where you were!" I said.

"Isn't that weird?" said Amber. "It just, like, magically appeared! Like the universe wanted him here!"

I hugged him again.

Only I knew it wasn't the universe.

It was me. And my wish.

And Gregory Grue, my fairy godmofo.

My opinion of Gregory changed in an instant.

"Come on," said Jason. "We're going to go bust into his old house. His parents still own it, so it ought to be empty."

Mutual smiled nervously.

"Okay," I said.

I didn't care where they were going, as long as I could go, too. I would have gone clear to St. Louis if they had just said the word.

We climbed into the car, Jason and Amber in the

front and Mutual and me in the back. I couldn't stop staring at him.

There was something weird about him. I mean, he was always sort of weird, but now something seemed to be bugging him. I hoped it wasn't me, but I couldn't help but wonder if maybe he was all disturbed that I was so much heavier now than I'd been six years ago. Or maybe he'd never seen a girl with purple hair.

Or maybe watching me go ape-crap with a crowbar on all those breakables had scared the heck out of him.

Maybe he was disappointed in me already.

And as he slumped down against the seat of the car and brushed the hair out of his eyes, I tried my hardest not to feel a little disappointed in *him*.

I had always imagined him swooping into town, kissing me, and saving me from my mundane life.

Now that he was here, he looked strong enough to save me from a polar bear, but he seemed . . . broken. More than I was, even.

There were lines in his face already, at the age of eighteen.

I kicked myself a bit—who looks like a knight in shining white armor after a three-thousand-mile trip? He had gone out of his way to try to contact me over the last six years, and now he was here.

How awful did I have to be to complain?

"I barely recognize Preston," Mutual said as we drove into town.

"It grew up," I said. "Once they built that new mall, the town grew up around us."

"Is Burger Baron still there?"

"No, thank God," said Amber. "That whole strip that used to be the main drag is gone. Everything but Yurkovich's Pizza."

Mutual's eyes lit up, probably for the first time since I'd seen him again. "Can we go there after we go to my house?" he asked.

"I insist on it," said Jason.

"I've been dreaming of getting a pizza for years," Mutual said.

Amber turned back toward me. "His parents kept him in, like, even more isolation in Alaska than they did here. But one time when they had to go into Anchorage, he shoplifted a bunch of music magazines and a copy of *The Complete Works of Shakespeare*. He's, like, figured out modern culture from those. Like how they can figure out half of what ancient Egypt was like from a handful of hieroglyphics."

Mutual blushed. "I also had a radio," he said. "That helped a lot. And I need to get some money, so I can mail it to the bookstore I ripped off."

"*Complete Works of Shakespeare?*" I asked with a smile.

He smiled, too.

"I reread *Henry the Fifth* on the trip," he said.

And he quoted a line from the St. Crispin's Day speech, one of the famous monologues from that play:

"'We few, we happy few, we band of brothers.'"

I smiled wider, and my disappointment started to evaporate. It wasn't quite as good as quoting that line about romance and youth's a stuff will not endure and pouncing on me, but it was a start.

It was enough to show me that he was still the awesome

guy I remembered. There were parts of him left inside, under the broken pieces I could see on the surface.

Maybe he was thinking the same thing about me.

He had already seen me as an extraordinary person, the kind I wanted to be, when we were eleven. I mean, the very fact that I read Shakespeare instead of a dictionary made me seem like a total bohemian to Mutual back then, just the way women in screwball comedies always seem to the cautious, buttoned-up guys who end up falling for them at the end of the movie.

Maybe love is all about finding someone who already sees you as the person you want to be, and can help you really get there.

When I looked out the window, I saw a car passing us. Gregory Grue was at the wheel—he gave me a little salute as he passed.

Just letting me know that he'd granted my wish, I guess. I smiled and saluted back, even though he was already out of sight.

Gregory Grue, I thought, *you're all right*.

Mutual Scrivener, the only guy I'd ever seriously liked who had definitely liked me back, had returned.

I couldn't believe I was sitting in a car with him.

And I liked the fact that he had come into town of his own accord when he got a ticket. That way I knew he wasn't just, like, under some sort of enchantment. He had come because he wanted to.

Jason drove out of Preston and into the farm country to the north, then, following Mutual's directions, turned onto a couple of back roads, heading into a wooded area.

I remembered that when I was younger, I thought there

was a place called the Faraway Woods. Every time you can see a long way in the distance around here, big groups of trees are visible along the horizon, but you never seem to drive through any forests in Iowa.

We were driving into one now.

While Amber and Jason filled me in on how Mutual had run away and dreamed about coming back, and while Mutual blushed and looked terrified, we drove deep into dark woods that I'd never seen before. It was spooky, really. I half expected to see mysterious little men playing nine-pins in the clearing. Actual fairies. Especially now that I knew magic was real.

Fairies, or something like them, were real. Not the kind who had been run out of forests and killed a few hundred years ago—Gregory must have been something else altogether.

Something new.

And he had chosen me.

I tried to make conversation with Mutual, even though what I really wanted to do was just kiss him and see if it, like, woke him up.

"Are you going to college in Iowa?" I asked.

"I hope so," he said. "But my parents' idea of home-schooling might not really be accredited."

"Oh, we'll get you taken care of," Amber said. "You can't tell me there was anyone in Alaska who was any smarter than you!"

"There was hardly anyone there to start with," he said.

"You can just take a GED exam," said Amber. "My uncle Larry passed that, and he can barely fart without an instruction manual."

We kept turning deeper into the forest until we came to a path that I never would have noticed if Mutual hadn't told Jason to turn down it. At the end of the path was a tiny house with weeds growing waist-high around it.

"Holy crap," said Jason. "Anyone else feel like we're about to get ambushed by the Vietcong?"

Amber turned back to Mutual. "Is this place haunted?" she asked. "It sure looks haunted."

"Not that I know of," said Mutual. "Unless some ghosts have moved in."

"Did you guys just abandon it?" I asked.

"Yeah," said Mutual. "One night about a week after you and I lost the district spelling bee, they told me to pack a bag. I loaded up some clothes and Jason's music player and that Paranormal Execution CD that he gave me, and the next morning I woke up in Alaska."

"How did they get from here to there so fast?" asked Amber.

Mutual didn't say anything. He just got out of the car and walked up to the house.

"I want to see how much got left behind," he said. "And if it's safe to stay here."

"You're staying *here*?" I asked.

"I can't afford a hotel," he said. "I'm broke."

I was about to offer to let him sleep on my couch (er, for now), but Jason broke in and beat me to the punch.

"We've had a spare room since my brother moved out," he said. "We'd be happy to have you. You can crash there."

"Would that be all right?" Mutual asked, his voice shaking more as he got closer to the house.

"Totally," said Jason.

I silently cursed myself for not offering him Val's old room.

You couldn't have possibly paid me enough to spend a night in Mutual's parents' old house. You couldn't even do it now, when I've lived through things a lot scarier than any ghost could ever be. I was half afraid that we'd open it up and find some witch who would shove us into the oven.

"Well, someone's been here," said Jason. "Look!"

There was a swear word scribbled in grime on one of the windows.

It was probably too dark for any of them to notice the smile on my face when I saw that.

The door was locked, so Mutual and Jason went to work kicking it in while Amber and I stood back.

"Nothing like watching your man destroy things," she said.

I just nodded and watched Jason doing his best to look like he was really helping, even though he wasn't nearly as strong as Mutual.

"He was asking about you, you know," said Amber. "He asked if you had a boyfriend. You should have seen how relieved he looked when we told him you didn't."

I smiled.

"He seems a lot more . . . worldly . . . now," said Amber. "I mean, he knows the facts of life and stuff. But he still seems like he just broke out of jail and hasn't figured out how to live on the outside. He could only learn so much from Shakespeare, classic rock radio, and a stack of magazines."

I snorted. "You can learn everything from Shakespeare."

"Not *everything*," she said. "Not, like, microwaves and text messaging."

"Point taken."

Jason and Mutual successfully broke the door open, and we all stepped into the old house.

Inside, it was scary as hell. There were probably spiders the size of Gregory Grue running around. It was dark, but I could see that there was a lot of dust covering every cabinet.

"Pretty much how you remembered it?" asked Jason.

"Yeah," said Mutual. "I guess they must have come back and cleaned it out or something. Either that or we got robbed. But there wasn't much worth stealing."

"How could they come back without you knowing?" I asked. "Did they leave you alone for weeks at a time?"

He didn't answer.

I wandered into the kitchen, where a tiny bit of starry light left from the sky was peeking in through a window. I was about to ask again how his parents could have come back when I opened a cabinet door and found three cans of VS32, the vegetable compound vampires drank instead of blood.

That explained how they could have come back so fast. They ran.

"Hey, Mutual," I said. "Were the vegetables you grew . . . for the compound?"

He stepped into the kitchen and took a deep breath.

"Mostly they sold them," he said, in a voice barely above a whisper. "But yeah, they kept enough to make their own. They didn't like the store-bought stuff much."

"Holy crap," said Amber. "Your parents are vampires?"

Mutual shuffled his feet. "I thought you'd probably already

figured that out. They're a pretty obvious case, when you think about it."

"Victorians?" I asked.

He nodded.

That explained a lot about their distaste for anything that didn't remind them of the good old days.

"I never found out much about their past," he said. "I don't know if they converted before or after the compound was discovered, so . . ."

"Gotcha," I said.

He wasn't sure if they'd ever killed anyone.

And I thought having to live with a dad who had broken into a school to get an answer sheet, like my dad did once, was psychologically damaging. At least I didn't have to wonder whether he had ever killed anyone to drink their blood.

"I didn't even know about them when I was a kid," he said.

"You didn't notice that your parents never got older?" asked Amber.

Mutual shrugged. "Who notices that when they're a little kid?"

I followed him into his old bedroom, where he dug around under the bed but didn't seem to find anything.

"That was why we moved. They knew the announcement that vampires were real was coming, and they wanted us to be even more isolated."

"I always thought it was because you didn't qualify for the state spelling bee," I said.

He smiled a bit. "That's what I thought, too, at first. I mean, people were getting crazy."

As I said, people in Preston used to take the spelling bees *really* seriously, and when none of us went on to the state finals, they weren't happy. There were For Sale signs in my yard, and, since Mutual wasn't really *from* Preston, there were a lot of rumors that he was a "traitor" who had been paid by larger schools to take a dive.

I did not miss the old, small-town version of Preston at all.

But the truth is, we *did* take a dive at the district bee. I guess I can admit it now that old-school Prestonians who bear grudges are about the least of my concerns.

It wasn't because anyone paid us, though. We had reason to believe that our lousy principal was rigging the bee so that he could take all the credit when we won. We decided that taking a dive was the right thing to do, even though it wrecked the spelling career that Mutual's parents had basically groomed him for.

It took a lot of guts on his part.

And it created a bond between the two of us. Even more so than the one I had with Jason and Amber, really, since they weren't in the district bee with us. But in their case, we'd had years to let our friendship grow. I knew them as well as I could imagine knowing anyone.

With Mutual, I still felt the bond, but on the other hand, he sort of seemed like a stranger.

Mutual sifted through some empty drawers, then said, "You know what? There's nothing here. Let's just go get a pizza."

He seemed deep in thought as Jason carefully steered his car down the narrow path that took us back to the road.

"So, you just turned eighteen?" I asked.

Mutual nodded.

"Do they want you to convert?"

He nodded again. "I was hoping to find the letter of intent they signed for me when I was little," he said, "so I could destroy it. But it's not there."

When vampires reproduce, the baby is a normal human. But the vampire community tends to put them under a *lot* of pressure to convert as soon as they turn eighteen. It's one of the horrible things that some of them think is okay because "that's what vampires do."

Like I said: Worst. Excuse. Ever.

"They had someone lined up to do it to me—a friend of theirs." Mutual shuddered. "A middle-aged woman who lived sort of near us out there. And they said I should think of it as a medical procedure, but she's no doctor. It makes me want to puke just thinking about her."

He turned away and looked out the window at the trees and the moonlight.

No human knew exactly how the conversion process worked, but it wasn't like getting a shot or a bite in the neck. It was said to be awfully intimate.

The very idea of someone being that intimate with him—well, someone other than me—made me want to break something. I only had a mental image of what the woman looked like, but I imagined shredding her in one of those big wood chippers that would spray chunks of her all over the Alaska snow.

"How long will it take them to get here if they run?" asked Jason.

"Couple hours," Mutual said. "Tops. And I'm pretty sure they're planning a diciotto."

"What's a diciotto?" asked Jason.

"It's where vampire parents get a bunch of vampires into a room and sort of brainwash their eighteen-year-old offspring into consenting to convert," I said. "They call it a rite of passage, but it's really barbaric."

"And it almost always works," said Mutual. "I think they sort of hypnotize you into thinking you're worthless unless you're a vampire or something."

"Think you could handle it if they did one on you?" I asked.

"That's part of why I came here," he said. "I was never braver than I was when I was with you guys."

I smiled over at him.

"I might be able to help," I said. "I'm in the Iowa Human/Post-Human Alliance. There are vampires there who might be able to protect you. I know at least one of them has tried to lobby the council to outlaw diciottos."

Mutual inched a little bit over toward me in his seat.

I had always imagined him showing up again and saving me from my life of mediocrity. Teaching me to be 100 percent alive.

Obviously, that wouldn't be happening.

He needed *me* to save *him*.

When we got to Yurkovich's Pizza, I had hoped he would wander in looking like he could hear the secrets of the universe in the sound of the bubbling grease, in the glow of the dim yellow lights, and in the stains on the threadbare carpet, the way Shakespeare could find layers of meaning in the grime on the London streets. But he still seemed quiet, shy, and afraid.

At least now I understood why he was afraid—diciottos were scary business.

As we ate, I noticed another swear word scrawled in the window of Yurkovich's and smiled. Gregory had been here.

Gregory Grue might have been a disgusting slob who was lacking in social graces, but I owed him a lot.

He had granted my wish.

After they dropped me off at home, Mom was sitting up in the kitchen.

"Well," she said, "it appears that we need to talk."

"What?" I asked.

I assumed she had somehow found out about the traffic ticket, which already seemed like it had happened ages ago, not a few hours ago.

"I got a call from Marcy Keyes," she said. "She told me that boy with the weird name I can never remember is back in town."

I smiled. "Yeah," I said. "Mutual."

And I told her all about Mutual—how he'd been basically imprisoned in Alaska, partly as punishment for not winning a spelling bee. She shook her head disapprovingly the whole time.

"What makes you think he's going to grow into a person you still like?" she asked. "Maybe he'll turn into a real jerk. Maybe he'll discover other girls. Sounds like he's attractive enough that you'll probably have competition."

"No way," I said. "That can't happen."

"I just don't want you to get hurt, Jennifer," Mom said. "Or to end up like Val, thinking every new boy is the one to change your life for. Or to get your hopes up."

"I won't," I said.

"Looks to me like you already have," she said. "Just be careful."

And she left me at the table.

I almost wished I had something left to smash.

If you ask me, Mom hadn't quite gotten over the idea that Mutual was competition for me or something. She had known that Mutual and I liked each other (just like everyone else in town had) and hadn't approved, and I guess she hadn't stopped to think that things were different now. We weren't going against each other for a spot at the state spelling bee anymore.

And why shouldn't I have a boyfriend? I deserved one as much as anyone else, and Mutual and I had been brought together by magic. Actual magic!

But she sort of had a point, as much as I hated to admit it.

For one thing, no one else had liked him when we were eleven. He was a total dork, and there were barely half a dozen other girls in class to start with. I might have more competition now that he was totally cut.

Also, I didn't really know Mutual that well. No one did. Not even him. There was no telling what kind of person he'd turn out to be away from his parents. I hoped he wasn't just going to be shy, retiring, and muttering all the time now.

But hell—I hadn't really figured myself out yet, either.

My life until a month or two before hadn't been lugging

giant vegetables around a farm with no phone, TV, or Internet connection, but it probably left me with even less free time than he had.

We were both free now—or freer than we'd ever been.

We might not have figured out who we were yet, but we would. And we could help each other.

And I was willing to bet that he'd turn out to be someone I still wanted to know. Probably someone I still wanted to kiss.

If we could just get me through the weekend, and him through the diciotto.

As I lay in bed, I hummed a few verses of "Goodnight, My Someone" from *The Music Man*. It wasn't the song I had to learn, but it seemed more appropriate at the moment.

Goodnight, my someone, goodnight.

Jenny couldn't believe that *this* was Mutual. The boy with a designer backpack, the coolest clothes, and the best batting average in Little League had grown into a teenager with a bowl cut. He seemed like he had forgotten to take the hanger out of his blazer before putting it on.

In short, he had grown up to be a nerd.

A nerd who wanted a kiss—and expected to get it!

ten

Yep. Exactly the opposite.

I had never, in my wildest dreams, imagined that he would grow up to be so . . . dreamy. Rugged.

He was pale and scared and a little unkempt, and not exactly acting like a knight in shining armor so far, but I could just imagine that once he cleaned himself up, he'd look as if he were on the cover of a romance novel.

After all, he had to be jet-lagged, in addition to worrying about being brainwashed into agreeing to be turned into a vampire.

I wasn't really the most empathetic person alive or anything (something I've worked on since then), but I could see where all of *that* could get you down.

In the morning at school, I went straight to the theater to thank Gregory for granting my wish, but he wasn't around yet. I guessed he was only in for one period a day.

Cathy was sulking around in the hall by her locker, and even shaking Fred off when he tried to comfort her. When she saw me, she gave me the dirtiest look anyone had ever given me.

It hurt. I might not have been popular, exactly, but people didn't usually hate me enough to give me dirty looks like that. Most people seemed to like me, even. I didn't enjoy having enemies.

I walked up to Cathy, hoping I could settle things with her.

"Hey," I said.

"Get away from me," she said.

"Look," I said, "I didn't ask for any part in the show. I don't want it. I'm going to tell Gregory to give it back to you."

"I have a meeting with the little freak today," she said. "I'll handle him."

"Want me to come along? I'll take your side."

She shook her head. "Just leave me alone."

I shrugged and walked off.

I really didn't want the part. The mayor's wife doesn't sing much, but, well, it was still more singing than I was going to be able to pull off. Some people really do come alive onstage, but I'm not one of those people.

I was just getting to my locker when Amber tapped me on the shoulder.

"There you are!" she said. "Where've you been?"

"I was trying to find the new director," I said.

"And I was trying to find *you*! We stayed up, like, all night talking to Mutual last night."

I tried not to let on how jealous I was to have been left out of that.

"He's, like, the coolest guy ever now," she said. "Did you ever hear of aerial hunting?"

"Is that where they kill wolves and stuff with airplanes?"

"Yeah. There was an airport base a mile from his ranch— he used to sneak out there at night and steal parts of the airplanes so they couldn't take off!"

Swoon.

"Awesome!" I said. "He was like a superhero!"

She leaned in closer. "And when *we* told him that, he said he was just imagining what *you* would have wanted him to do. You inspired him, Jennifer."

I smiled.

Well, actually, no. I made a noise like "Squee!"

I hadn't seen much of it yet myself, but there was definitely some evidence that he wasn't as much of a cowering wreck as he'd seemed to be the night before, if he was out engaging in espionage.

"And it gets better," she said. "We're going on a double date tonight. *Date*. Jason specifically referred to it as a date."

"Please tell me you're not kidding," I said. "Because if you are, you'll be missing several vital organs in the morning."

"Didn't it feel good, the four of us all together again?" asked Amber. "We just, like, fit. We could retire together and buy condos in the same senior apartment complex."

"Let's not get ahead of ourselves," I said.

But I was imagining it, too. I was imagining Mutual and me as adults. We'd live in a small, colorful apartment next door to a theater, with the million or so of his babies I planned to have, and we'd be mild-mannered liberal arts professors by day and environmental espionage agents by night. Everyone would think we were a couple of extraordinary people.

I also knew I was still imagining myself with the version of Mutual that I'd always wanted him to be. I had to accept the fact that the real one might not live up to it.

But I spent all day drawing little sketches of Mutual in the margins of my notes. If the favor I owed Gregory was kissing Mutual at the dance, I was more than ready for the challenge. No way was I letting him come back to town without getting the kiss we'd planned for all those years ago.

When I got to the auditorium for fourth-period rehearsal, I found Gregory Grue sitting on a stool onstage, talking to Eileen Codlin, who was taking notes. All of a sudden (and this is the only time I ever, ever thought this), I really couldn't wait to read her book. I wanted to know more about this fairy godparent business.

I walked down the aisle and hopped onto the stage.

"Hey," I said to Gregory.

"Hoo hoo," said Gregory, in a more casual tone than usual. "Did you work on your song this weekend?"

"Some," I said. "But I really just wanted to thank you."

"For the part? Don't thank me, just rehearse! If you suck, it'll make me look bad."

"No," I said. "For . . . you know. Granting my wish."

"I didn't grant any wishes yet," he said. "I've gotten you off to a good start, but these things take time. And you still owe me a favor with a guy to be named later."

"Doesn't look like it'll be a problem," I said.

"Is this how fairy magic works?" asked Eileen.

"It's like this, baby," said Gregory to Eileen. "As soon as one of us decides to grant someone a couple of wishes, it creates this vacuum of energy in the world that can only be filled by having the wisher do us a little favor. Nothing much. I wish we could do away with that whole angle, but I don't make the rules."

He looked over at me and said, "Remember that. I don't make 'em. I just follow 'em."

"Sure," I said.

"Now go backstage and talk to whoever's in charge of costumes."

"Actually," I said, "I was going to ask if you could give the part back to Cathy. She wants it a lot more than I do."

"The play's the thing, kiddo," he said. "My job here is to make this show the best it can be, and you've got the right look for the mayor's wife, minus the Grimace hair, which we'll cover up. Cathy's all wrong for it. Mrs. Alison must have been drinking from an extra-large water bottle the day she did the casting!"

"Can't you fix her with makeup?"

"Look, I have a meeting with her right after class. Just let the two of us work all this out, and keep your nose on your own face, where it belongs, okay?"

"Sure."

I thought I'd ask again later, and wandered around to find Marty, the guy who was in charge of costumes.

I wasn't in any of the scenes that were being rehearsed that day, so I sat back and watched as Cathy and the rest of the chorus worked on the blocking for the "Iowa Stubborn" number. Gregory directed like a tyrant, shoving people around and yelling if they took a step with the wrong foot.

Under normal circumstances, I would have thought he was being a real dick.

But in my haze of stupidity, I thought he was simply being a really passionate director.

Right before my last class of the day, I stepped into the hall and saw Cathy yelling at Fred.

"I hate you!" she shouted. "I never want to talk to you again! Get away from me!"

Fred looked shocked.

Cathy threw a textbook at him. Being a vampire, he had no trouble getting out of the way. It landed on the floor and slid down the hall toward me.

When it got to my feet, Cathy gave me a look I couldn't quite place and said, "Why don't *you* go out with him instead?"

A crowd gathered around the two of them.

"What are you all looking at?" Cathy shouted. "Mind your own business!"

"Can't we just talk?" asked Fred.

Cathy screamed out a swear word.

Mrs. Smollet appeared out of nowhere, took Cathy by the arm, and led her away.

Fred stood there in the hall, staring and looking aghast. He didn't even move when the bell rang.

I asked around a bit but couldn't quite get the story out of anyone. No one seemed to have seen the whole thing.

But by the end of the day, the pieces had been put together.

All through fifth period, Cathy had been telling Fred she wanted to break up and that he should go date some other girl. He had sort of resisted, until she blew up in the hall.

Word had it that it all started when he told her he didn't want to convert her after all, but no one was sure.

All we knew was that she'd be spending the rest of the week in in-school suspension.

"What am I going to do about Mutual?" asked Jenny hopelessly. "Even my purple hair doesn't bother him. I just know he's going to kiss me tonight! I don't want my first kiss to be with *him*! I want it to be *special*! And I want it to make me a princess!"

"I have an idea," said her fairy god-mother. "Just let me take out my wand. . . ."

eleven

Unless you're awfully dumb, you can probably guess that I never had my fairy godmother give me acne and the ability to spray some nasty-smelling mist, like a skunk, to scare Mutual away, like she does in the book. That would have just been plain mean, even if I didn't like him. The "Jenny" in the book should have been nicer to Mutual, even if he was annoying, and maybe even something of a stalker whose attempts to kiss her could be considered sexual harassment by most courts.

Girls, if you're being harassed, the thing to do is get a lawyer. Not turn into a weird half-girl, half-skunk creature to gross your stalker out. Remember: it didn't work for "Jenny."

I might not have looked like a model or anything on the night of my date with Mutual, but I can guarantee you that I didn't stink. I took the longest shower of my life and used up half of my products. Then I spent much longer than usual picking out an outfit. I wanted something sexy, but not, like, so slutty that I'd scare him off. At least it had warmed up enough that I could just wear a jacket and not have to worry about looking like Grimace in a giant coat. The ice had melted, leaving us with deep puddles full of soggy November leaves.

When I drove out to Jason's, I felt positively elated. I had forgotten all my disappointment that Mutual wasn't acting like some sort of Superman, and shoved the voice in my head reminding me of the difference between the real Mutual and the fantasy one into its own compartment where I couldn't hear it.

This was the night I'd been waiting for all my life. The day that made my life up until that point worth it.

I could think of every bad thing that had ever happened to me—every bad day, every time my crowded schedule seemed to be keeping me from having a social life, everything—and how it had led me to this place.

Mutual came out of Jason's house wearing a plain black T-shirt and looking even more nervous than usual. I was nervous, too.

Jason got into the backseat and motioned Mutual into the front.

"Hi, Mutual," I said.

"Hi," he said. He was blushing already. It was pretty cute, really.

We drove out to Amber's parents' ranch to pick her up, and she promptly made out with Jason a little bit, kicking my seat in the process to get my attention and suggest that it might be a good time for Mutual and me to do the same.

Mutual and I looked at each other, but we both just sort of smiled nervously, and I started to drive.

"Did you ever go into downtown Des Moines when you lived in Preston?" I asked.

"Not that I remember," he said. "As far as I know, my first time there was yesterday, when I took the cab from there to Jason's. I think it's about the same size as Anchorage, though. I went there a couple times. And all the radio stations came out of there."

Man, it was weird to hear him using contractions.

Jason passed me up a tape he'd made of old metal songs that Mutual knew—my car only had a tape player. I didn't really know any of the songs myself, but hearing Mutual and Jason sing along at the top of their lungs was fun.

Between songs, Mutual threw back his head and laughed. He seemed as though he was finally coming up for air after being underwater for years—like he was coming out of his shell, just the way I'd hoped he would.

"Oh wow," he said. "I could never cut loose like that at the farm. I had to listen to the radio really quietly on headphones that I hid under my mattress. I never got to sing along!"

"You have a good voice," I said. "You could totally be a singer."

"Beats being a speller," Jason said. "You get a lot more groupies, too. I don't think there's such a thing as spelling groupies."

Amber elbowed him in the ribs.

"What's a groupie, exactly?" Mutual asked.

Jason leaned up and whispered in his ear, and Mutual blushed a bit.

"Oh," he said. "I don't really need any of those, though."

I smiled.

"Neither does Jason," Amber pointed out.

"That word wasn't in the dictionaries?" Jason asked.

"Mine weren't exactly unabridged," he said. "Remember how Marianne Cleaver used to pick on me because my dictionary wasn't big enough?"

"All boys worry that they should have a bigger dic . . . tionary," said Jason.

We all cracked up, though it took Mutual a second to get the joke. He'd obviously come a long way since the days when he'd worn a blazer, a belt, *and* suspenders and had a bowl cut, but he still had a lot to learn.

And I couldn't wait to teach him.

"So," I said. "I want to hear about this thing where you stopped people from aerial hunting!"

He shrugged. "I didn't really stop anyone," he said. "The airport was a half-hour hike from my house, so I could sneak out there in the middle of the night and unscrew wheels and stuff and get back before my parents noticed I was gone. But it's not like they couldn't just replace the parts I stole."

"That's still awesome!" I said.

He shrugged again. "I needed to do something for excitement. But no matter what you do it for, unscrewing wheels isn't terribly exciting."

"Neither is spelling," I said. "And look at the mess *that* got us into back in the day."

"Do people still remember that around here?" he asked.

I shook my head. "Nah. Once the vampires came out of the coffin, everyone forgot all about it," I said. "I would have, too, except that I couldn't forget about you."

He blushed again.

I got onto the interstate and headed toward downtown Des Moines.

Unless you're one of the people who's been camping out on my lawn, odds are that you've never been to Des Moines. We're not exactly a vacation spot. If you like giant umbrella statues, we're your place—we've got one of those outside of the Civic Center. A giant fiberglass cow, too, outside of the dairy on East University. Other than that, there's not much here that you can't find in any other city, except maybe George the Chili King, the greasy spoon on Hickman Road.

It may not be an exciting place to visit, but it's a great place to live. We have a nice downtown that feels like a real city these days, but you're never more than a fifteen-minute drive from rolling hills of green fields, if that's what you're into. We have nice parks, theaters, and farmers' markets. There are band concerts on the steps of the capitol building in the summer.

The commutes here are short, too. Preston is just about the farthest suburb from downtown, and we were almost there in twenty minutes.

The lights in the big buildings on the horizon were like extra stars—I liked looking at the patterns formed by the windows that had lights on and the ones that didn't. It was sort of like looking for pictures in the craters on the moon.

"Hey," said Amber. "Check out the Weather Beacon. It's purple."

The Weather Beacon is this big pole covered in lights that you can see from all over town. If the lights are white, it means it's going to get colder. If they're red, it's getting warmer and if they're green, there's no change coming. There's a rhyme to explain it that I can never quite remember.

This night, it was glowing purple.

"What the hell?" asked Jason. "What does that mean?"

"I don't know," said Amber. "And how are they going to work that into the rhyme? Nothing rhymes with purple."

"Nurple," said Jason.

"Don't you dare," she giggled, slapping his hand.

I was pretty sure I knew what it meant when the Weather Beacon was purple.

It meant that my fairy godparent wanted me to know this was *my* night.

Even the Jenmobile was running better than usual. We had made it almost all the way downtown before it stalled out. I put it into neutral and let it roll to the side of the road.

"Sorry, guys," I said. "This happens a lot. We'll be fine in ten minutes."

"This is why we don't have flying cars," said Jason. "One of *those* things stalls and you're dead!"

"I haven't been in too many cars," said Mutual, "but they don't usually have a dashboard like this, do they?"

My dashboard was made out of carved wood—it was like an art project for whoever had owned it before.

"Nope," I said. "It's the main reason I bought the car. I probably should have sprung for one with a good engine instead, though."

"I like it," said Mutual. "It's not like any other car."

"Exactly," I said.

"We're right by a cemetery," said Amber. "Isn't this the

one where Alley Rhodes and her zombie boyfriend got attacked?"

"I think so," I said. "Prom was at the Science Center that year, and that's right by us."

"I hear his grave is, like, a shrine now," said Jason. "People who think Alley and Doug were tragic lovers or something make pilgrimages to it."

"Tragic lovers?" Amber scoffed. "I doubt it. Did you ever read any of Alley's old columns from the school paper? She was vicious!"

"I've never read them," I said, "but I've met her a few times since she graduated. She comes to alliance meetings during the summer, when she's in town."

"What's she like?" asked Amber.

I shrugged. "She doesn't seem that mean to me," I said. "Maybe she's settled down. Maybe falling in love was just what she needed."

"Maybe," said Amber.

I turned to Mutual. "Did you hear about that? The first vampire attack in about a hundred and fifty years was right here in Des Moines."

"I heard," he said. "It was on the radio. That Wilhelm guy sounds pretty awful."

"He was an awful drummer, I can tell you that much," said Jason. "I saw that band he was in at the Cage one time, and they could have sucked a walnut through a straw."

"Every time there's a dance, people say his clan is going to come get revenge, just because he attacked Alley at the prom," said Amber. "Stupid."

"Is his clan still around?" asked Mutual.

"They've been told never to show their faces around here again," I said. "They got banished to Canada's great outdoors."

"You two should go see the grave," said Amber. "See if it's really a shrine."

She gave the back of my seat a kick, which meant "you two should go be alone together."

I looked over at Mutual. "You want to?"

"I will if you will," he said. He turned back to Jason and Amber. "Are you guys coming?"

"I think they want some time to make out in the back-seat," I said.

The two of us got out of the car.

The gates of the cemetery were locked—they're always locked. It's the law now, actually—all cemeteries are on lock-down in case anyone has cast the zombie rites over any graves. Zombies are usually pretty harmless, but the first few hours after they rise up, they're sort of in frenzy mode. Keeping them locked into the cemetery is safer for every-one, including the zombies. If they rise up behind a locked fence, they're less likely to get machine-gunned by a hill-billy.

"So, how do people get in?" I asked.

"There's probably a broken link in the fence someplace," said Mutual. "Let me see."

He began to run his hand along the gates, and then found a space where the boards were farther apart than most of the others. There was just enough room for us to shimmy through, though I really had to squeeze.

"You okay?" he asked as I pushed through.

"I've got it," I said.

"This is a pretty safe place to be," he said. "My parents wouldn't attack around so many other people's graves."

Vampires can't go into other people's graves, for some reason. Most of them avoid cemeteries altogether. Just being in a place this comparatively safe seemed to loosen Mutual up a bit. He stopped looking over his shoulder every few seconds and started to smile.

You might say he really came alive in the graveyard.

We walked through the grounds, and I said, "'Tis now the very witching time of night, when churchyards yawn.'"

Hamlet.

Mutual smiled and countered with, "'Now it is the time of night that the graves, all gaping wide, every one lets forth his sprite, in the church-way paths to glide.'"

"Spooky," I said. "What's that from?"

"*Midsummer Night's Dream.*"

It wasn't hard to spot Doug's grave—I remembered Alley saying he had liked to build stuff, and from the looks of things, he had really tricked out his gravestone. There was a huge wooden carving built on top of the stone marker, as easy to spot as the Weather Beacon in the skyline, even in the dark graveyard.

As we walked up toward it, I started to feel, like, overwhelmed. There was this . . . feeling in the air that I walked right into. I didn't understand what it was. Maybe what had happened that night, when Doug crumbled to dust (right in his own grave, which was kind of convenient, I guess) in Alley's arms, had left some kind of energy in the space around his grave.

That didn't seem scientifically sound, but I felt what I felt. I didn't feel spooked, like I should have in a graveyard at night. I felt sadness and love.

The grave was really a sight to see. All around it, people had left little tokens—teddy bears, candy, beer bottles. People had even written their names and lines of songs and stuff on the stone part, like on that one rock star's grave in Paris.

"Wow," Mutual said. "This is, like, where he actually died, too, right? The second time he died?"

"Yeah," I said.

We lingered for a while, reading all the lines from songs people had scribbled.

"Break on through to the other side, Doug."

"There is a crack in everything,
that's how the light gets in."

"Romeo and Juliet are together in eternity."

"What kind of price do you have to pay to get out of
going through all these things twice."

"Are these all song lyrics?" Mutual asked.

"I think so," I said. "I don't really know many of them."

"I recognize some of them from the radio," he said. "I wish I could write songs like that. The kind that hit you so hard you want to write the lyrics on gravestones."

"I'll bet you could."

We stood over the grave.

I crouched down and put my hand in the graveyard dirt.

"I can feel it," I said. "All the stuff Doug must have been feeling."

"The pain?"

"Sort of," I said as we stepped right up to the grave itself. "I feel like I can feel everything the two of them were feeling that night. Sadness. Love. Sadness, mostly."

I felt it, all right.

Along with a desperate urge not to let a minute of my life go to waste.

"Do you remember the last time we saw each other?" he asked. "Before my parents moved me away?"

Oh God. Here it was.

"Yeah," I said. "We made an appointment to meet up the next day in the wooded area between the playground and the street."

"To kiss," he said.

"Yeah. To kiss."

We stared at each other and giggled a bit.

"Such a sixth-grade thing to do. Scheduling a kiss. Most people just *do* it, you know?"

"Yeah," he said. "Well . . . sorry I'm so late."

"You're here now," I said. "So, are we going to keep the appointment?"

"If you don't want to cancel," he said.

"Nope."

I shook my head and smiled. For a split second, I was glad that I'd put on weight. If I was still as skinny as I'd been at eleven, the butterflies in my stomach might have picked me up and carried me clear away.

I took a step closer to him.

Then Mutual stepped closer to me.

And then we kissed.

My eyes were closed, but I'm almost sure, even now that I think back on it, that if I'd opened my eyes, there would have been purple fireworks going off in the background.

Jenny had never been kissed, but she had often imagined what her first kiss would be like—her lips pressed against the lips of a gorgeous boy, melting into him like warm butter as the tips of their tongues gently brushed. Feeling their souls touch as her purple hair flowed over his shoulders like the warm glow of the streetlight flooding the pavement on the streets outside the gym.

twelve

That was how I had imagined it, too. And I still imagined it that way, even though I had been kissed once, at least technically.

My first kiss, the truth-or-dare kiss, was nothing like that. During that kiss, I felt like we were both pulling away the whole time. And our lips were both so tightly clenched that it was like kissing a rock for me—and probably for him, too.

And, honestly, the tiny kiss I had with Mutual at Doug the Zombie's grave wasn't a whole lot better. His lips were soft, but it was just a quick peck, really.

Still, it was more than enough for me.

I felt everything "Jenny" imagined.

When I stepped back, I was smiling so wide that it made my cheeks hurt.

I was the girl who took ice skates to school, saw pictures made of windows, and had her first real kiss while standing over the grave of a zombie.

And who then turned cartwheels through the cemetery.

Yeah, after the quick peck I was so elated that I couldn't quite stand still. I let forth a "squee" and turned a cartwheel, which was something I hadn't tried since I was a good forty pounds lighter.

Mutual followed along, laughing at my attempt at acrobatics.

"Okay, smarty," I said. "Let's see what you got."

And he turned a cartwheel. A perfect one.

He certainly showed me.

When I tried to do another one, I slipped on a wet leaf and ended up falling on my butt.

He reached a hand down to pull me up, but instead I pulled him down to the dirty ground next to me and giggled. I moved over a bit more to cuddle up next to him. Wet leaves clung to me—they smelled like cinnamon and nutmeg.

I wouldn't say I felt like I had become the extraordinary person I had always wanted to be, but I was a lot closer to feeling like I'd actually been that way all along.

"That looked painful," he said.

I shrugged. "Did you know I used to shove snow down my boots when I was a kid?" I asked him.

"Why?"

"I liked it to freeze my ankles so badly that they hurt, so it would feel even better when I got to warm up at home."

He nodded. "Makes sense," he said. "I guess."

"Sort of like having to wonder where you were all this time hurt, but it just makes having you back feel even better now."

I moved my hand down into his and squeezed, interlocking our fingers. Then I kissed him again, better and slower this time.

Then he kissed me, long and hard and good. Just the way I'd imagined he would for years.

It was a wish come true, all right.

I never wanted to stop kissing him. Ever.

He smiled between kisses. "You kiss just right," he said, "like only a lonely angel can."

I kissed him quickly. "Is that Shakespeare?"

He shook his head. "Springsteen. Heard it on the classic rock station."

I laughed and we kissed again.

I suppose it was kind of an ego boost for him to see me react like that to being kissed by him, because any trace of nervousness he had was gone. We sat on the ground and kissed and held hands and talked about everything and nothing. We made some plans to see about getting him into Drake.

Maybe it sounds kind of ridiculous to think that after a few minutes of kissing, I really couldn't ever imagine myself with anyone else, but I couldn't. I think maybe you never can in the middle of making out with someone you like, but still. I felt different with him.

We kissed and cuddled until we got too cold, then headed back through the damp grass of the graveyard, with the Weather Beacon glowing purple above us. Jason and Amber were still in the backseat of the Jenmobile, looking sort of disheveled.

"Hey, guys," I said. "Have you been turning my car into a den of sin?"

"We might ask you the same question about Doug's grave!" said Amber.

I laughed and got in the driver's seat.

"So, tell me," said Amber. "Yes or no?"

"Yes," I said, as we deluded ourselves that *maybe* Jason and Mutual didn't know what we meant.

Amber squealed and kicked my seat. I think she was almost as excited as I was.

My car started right back up, and we headed into downtown for dinner at the Noire Cafe (which had been a goth-themed restaurant a while before, but had turned into a nice Italian place now that the goth craze had settled down), then drove around to see the sights of Des Moines. Which, again, mostly add up to a giant umbrella statue and a big fiberglass cow.

But I liked both of those, and Mutual seemed impressed. He was impressed by everything. I don't want to say he was seeing layers and layers of meaning in everything, like Shake-speare, but he almost seemed like he was.

This was the Mutual I'd been waiting for.

"Where to now?" I asked when it got to be about ten o'clock. I'd never gone out enough for my mom to bother giving me a curfew, and Jason wasn't in the habit of honoring his. I didn't want the night to end.

"Wherever," said Amber.

"What do people usually do at this hour, anyway?" I asked. "Besides go to strip clubs or bars or parties in people's basements."

"Sometimes my coworkers and I go play Pac-Man at the coin laundry place after work," said Jason.

"Pac-Man?" I said.

"Yeah," he said. "You know, the video game."

"Yes, I know what Pac-Man is. But why?"

"They have one of the old machines at this one laundry place on Merle Hay Road that's open all night," said Jason. "We go out there at, like, midnight to play Pac-Man, drink cans of pop, and talk to whoever's there."

"What kind of people do you meet in a coin laundry at midnight?" I asked.

"Weirdos, mostly," he said. "Night owls. That and people whose washing machines are on the fritz."

"Sounds good to me," I said. "Want to head over there?"

"Sure," said Jason. "Only it might be too crowded. Like, half the restaurant industry goes there to party after work now. My crew was into it back before it was cool, though."

Amber laughed. "I love it," she said. "You were into *Pac-Man* before it was cool!"

"Well, okay, we were into it about thirty years after the first time it was cool," he said. "But before it got cool again."

"When it was just you and the nighthawks at the coin laundry," I said.

I pulled onto Merle Hay Road, and Jason pointed me over to a laundry place near Douglas Avenue. Inside, there were about four people doing laundry. I thought they might be hippies, but it was hard to tell if they were bohemians or just kind of dirty.

Jason changed a twenty in the bill slot and bought us all grape sodas from a vending machine, and we gathered around the Pac-Man game.

I watched Jason go through a game first (he was pretty good), and then watched Amber play (she sucked), and sort of got the hang of it by observing. If you're a quick study, Pac-Man is not the hardest game to master. When it was my turn, I knew what to do.

It was a fun way to cap off an evening, and the grape soda was a nice touch. Purple stuff, you know. It gave Mutual nice, grape-flavored breath (even though grape-flavored stuff does not taste remotely like grapes, or any other fruit that occurs in nature, for that matter).

I guided Mutual's arms around my waist. He still seemed a tiny bit shy about touching me or kissing me, and I wanted to get him over that as soon as possible.

Meanwhile, the radio was playing one Beatles song after another. Mutual said he'd heard most of them on the radio and sang along with the ones he knew.

I thought a bit about John Lennon. He was a pretty violent person at first, but with help from his wife, he became totally peaceful. If he could do it, I could. I was never as mean and sardonic as he was at my age.

Or Alley Rhodes, for that matter—people used to call her the Ice Queen of the Vicious Circle. But Doug had helped her change.

I might have been turning into a violent, bitter girl instead of the charming free spirit Mutual had seen me as when I was eleven. But I could change.

Between songs, the DJ came on.

"Weird night in Des Moines," he said. "In addition to the Weather Beacon, we're getting reports of purple stuff all over the place. We just had someone call and tell us that that statue of the naked angel on a tricycle down at the mall is also purple."

"Ha!" I said. "Tonight is the Feast of St. Jennifer the Purple!"

"Let's take some callers," the DJ said. "Caller, you're on the air."

"This is some kind of post-human crap," said the voice of a guy who sounded like a farmer. "Whole town's gone to hell since they all moved here."

"And let's not forget it's homecoming season," said the DJ. "I'm sure we've all heard the usual rumors that the vampire who attacked that girl three years ago is somehow still alive, or his clan is in town for revenge."

"They have to come sooner or later," said the caller.

"The president of the Human/Post-Human Alliance, whatever that is, has said that an 'honor guard of vampires' is on call to deal with any issues," the DJ said. "Call me crazy, but it doesn't make me feel much better."

"Is that your group?" Mutual asked me.

I nodded.

The next caller said that he thought painting things purple was something vampires did to celebrate after attacking someone, like how the Death Eaters in the Harry Potter books cast the Dark Mark whenever they kill.

"Man," I said. "I'm so sick of all this 'trouble with a capital T and that rhymes with P and that stands for post-humans' crap. I owe post-humans a lot, you know."

Mutual squeezed my hand.

I guess he thought I meant that if it weren't for his vampire parents, I wouldn't have him. Which was true.

But I actually meant my fairy godparent. Who was technically a *pre*-human, but, well, same difference.

He had painted the town purple just for me, and made my wish come true.

After three cans of grape pop, I excused myself to take a pee and found a swear word scrawled in the mirror of the ladies' room.

I stared at it for a second before opening the stall door to find Gregory Grue sitting on the toilet.

"*There* you are!" said Jenny, with a huge sigh of relief. "It looks like I can't possibly stink enough to make Mutual not want to kiss me. You've got to help!"

"Just let me take out my wand," her fairy godmother said. "You weren't meant to be with him. You were meant for an extraordinary life with Fred. You are going to be a princess. . . ."

thirteen

Most of you have probably figured out by now that the long-haired muscular guy you've seen pictures of is actually Mutual, not Fred, like we've been saying it is.

Yeah. We like to *tell* people Mutual is Fred, so they won't send him hate mail.

So you're also probably wondering what, exactly, Fred had to do with the whole story.

Well, it's coming up.

I jumped in shock when I saw Gregory sitting there, but I really wasn't scared so much as surprised to find him in the stall of the women's bathroom.

He was sitting on the toilet (with his pants up, thank God) holding a bottle of beer and reclining against the tank.

"Hoo hoo!" he said, raising the bottle like he was giving a toast. "It's a wonderful night for laundry! A wonderful night for drinks!"

"God!" I said. "You shocked me."

"I come like a mole and go like a weasel, kiddo," he said. "Happy?"

"Yes, thank you," I said. "I'm happier than I've ever been in my life."

He grinned, but it wasn't a happy grin. More of a wicked one.

"That's just swell, kiddo," he said. "But you know what? Two of your three wishes were for misery, not happiness. You wished for Corey to get rejected—which happened, by the way. That Emily girl wouldn't be caught dead with a guy who stank of granola."

Something in the way he was talking made me shiver.

"And let's not forget the thing that you were wishing for the hardest of all," he said. "For revenge on Cathy."

He took a sip of his beer, and I felt a chill, like a cold drink, run down *my* throat, too.

"So, giving me her part in the play was how you granted my wish, huh?"

"Just the start, girly girl," he said. "Oh, she's really gonna go through it. We People of Peace really aren't in the business of making people happy, you know. We didn't call *ourselves* the People of Peace—the humans in the villages did. It was sort of like saying 'nice doggie' to a dog you know is gonna bite your ankles. And you—you're just as bad as we are! You get three wishes, and two out of three are for other people to be miserable! Hoo hoo!"

I felt my insides starting to curl around inside me.

Because he was right.

It was just like me—the girl who smashed things and

spent half her time imagining the violent deaths of people who annoyed her—to wish for misery over happiness.

I didn't like where this was going.

"Now, for instance, did you ever hear about Cinderella?"

"Sure."

"You know how that story really went, right? Back before they cleaned it up for the cartoons? How her stepsisters cut their toes off to fit into the glass slipper, then got pecked to death by birds?"

I shook my head. I knew that all the old fairy tales used to be really gory before they got cleaned up and all, but I hadn't heard that one.

"And do you know why Cinderella had to be back by midnight or her coach would turn into a pumpkin?"

I shook my head again.

"It was because her fairy godmother was a dick!" he said triumphantly. "A dick who wanted to see the look on Cindy's face when the coach turned into a pumpkin and the dress turned back to rags right in front of the prince. We're all sort of bastards like that."

He smiled and looked terribly, horribly pleased with himself.

"But she married the prince in the end," I said.

"Sure," said Gregory. "Only that prince was about as charming as a wiry black hair on a toilet seat. Cindy spent the rest of her life scrubbing castle floors and squeezing out babies. When she had five girls in a row, and no boys, they got rid of her."

He dragged his finger across his neck.

"You're not going to make Cathy cut her toes off, are

you?" I asked. I might have been angry at her, but I wasn't *that* spiteful. I was willing to let her keep her toes and all.

Gregory just laughed.

"She'll still be intact if everyone plays ball, kiddo. But what you're going to do now is the favor I asked you for, which will twist the knife even farther inside her guts. You're going to get her boyfriend to kiss you at the dance. The guy you've been dreaming about!"

"*Fred?*"

"None other! That's the guy I want you to kiss."

"I assumed it was Mutual!"

He laughed. "It could have been," he said. "But you also wished for Cathy to be miserable, so I went with having you kiss her boyfriend. She'll see you kissing him and realize that you've taken everything from her—her part, her boyfriend, everything!"

"Oh God," I said.

"So if you think I'm being mean," he said, "remember— *you're* the one who wished for what you wished for. You brought it on yourself. You wouldn't have to kiss her boyfriend if you hadn't wished for her to be miserable."

"He's not her boyfriend anymore," I said. "They broke up this afternoon."

"I know," said Gregory, "but she's just mad at him. She didn't stop caring about him. I'd say they'll be back together in two weeks if he doesn't find someone new, which gives you a nice little window of opportunity. And if that dance ends and Fred hasn't kissed you on the dance floor, you'll die."

And he tossed some glitter above his head and let it rain

down onto him. Some fell through the space between his legs and into the toilet.

"Well, I unwish what I wished," I said. "I don't want to be a part of this deal."

"I *told* you that's not how it works," he said. "You don't get a choice here. I got you Mutual back, I saw to it that that other boy ended up miserable, and now I'm granting your wish of making Cathy Marconi suffer. Now you have to get her boyfriend to kiss you at the dance, or you'll die. Simple as that. Even if you go right back to Mutual at the end of the night, she'll still know you did it, and it'll haunt her forever!"

Gregory grinned and took a long chug of beer. My knees were shaking as he hopped down from the toilet and walked out of the stall, past me and over to the mirror, where he took off his hat and started dragging a comb across his greasy hair. Bits of grease actually came flying out like spittle splashing against the mirror. He ran his fingers through his hair, then smeared the grease on his overcoat before pulling a cigar from his pocket and lighting it.

And, for no good reason, he started to whistle and dance a little jig while I slumped back against the wall.

He sang a bit of "Bang Bang Lulu," the song he'd been singing at McDonald's. I sang "Goodnight, Ladies," which was the same tune, right along with him to keep from hearing too much of what he was singing (none of which could be printed in a book for this age group).

When he finished up a verse about a guy with no teeth, he stood in front of me with a more serious look on his face.

"Now, let me give it to you straight, kiddo," he said. "I'd

say the odds that you're going to get Fred to kiss you at the dance are somewhere between slim and zilch. So the minute the dance ends, you *will* die."

I very nearly barfed.

He took a long drag on his cigar and exhaled. This time I definitely saw faces in the smoke rings. They all looked like teenage girls. Some were in old-fashioned bonnets. One looked like she was from the 1940s, and one was a hippie. They looked like they were trying desperately to talk to me before they dissipated and vanished into the air, but no sound came out of their mouths.

"Those faces," I said. "Are those . . . ?"

"Yeah," he said. "Aren't they lovely? They all got their wishes, but they didn't keep their end of the deal. See the one in the bonnet? Her job was to count all the grains of rice in a bag. And the bag kept refilling itself! Ha!"

"That's terrible."

"But on the bright side," he said as the last of the smoke withered away, "there's another option for you."

His grin got even wider.

"What?" I asked.

"You can't really be killed if you're already dead," he said. "So if you want, I can arrange to have you made into a vampire ahead of time. You'll satisfy the void in the universe, and you'll still be able to walk the earth and kiss your boyfriend."

"I can't possibly convert," I said. "There's a whole process you have to go through before you can do the operation. You have to sign a letter of intent at least a week prior, and the dance is in a few days."

"Oh, I know that," he said. "You need a letter of *intent* a week ahead, then a letter of *consent* on the day of the conversion. But we can get you one of those when the time comes, and you signed the letter of intent on Friday."

"No I didn't!" I said.

"Sure you did." He pulled a sheet of paper out of the inside pocket of his overcoat. "You probably should have read the thing I had you sign when I dropped off the Wells Fargo Wagon, kiddo."

I felt my face starting to burn.

"I like to plan ahead," he said. "I can't use the magic I get for myself, so I have to find creative ways to make it pay. I have a vampire buddy who pays me very, very well to bring him girls he can convert legally. More than I'd make using magic for stock tips or to rob a bank."

He smiled again, used a paper towel to wipe his hands, then shoved it in his mouth and took a bite.

"Your buddy sounds like a sick bastard to me," I said. "What, does he get his kicks converting girls?"

Gregory swallowed. "It's like a spiritual thing for him," he said. "Like a missionary performing baptisms."

"Right," I said. "That operation isn't just dunking someone's head in the water."

He moved in closer, looking at me like Jason's old pet snake used to look at mice just before it leaped out and broke their necks so it could swallow them whole.

"You won't even have to feel it," he said. "I'll cast a little spell to put you to sleep, and then my vampire friend will take care of everything. You'll still die the minute the dance ends, but the death won't take, since you'll already be undead. It's either that or you can drop dead and stay that way. Your choice, kiddo."

Some choice. Dying on the spot or becoming a teenager

forever. Either way, my chances of ever being an extraordinary person were shot. You can't grow when your brain doesn't mature.

Gregory took another bite of his paper towel, then offered me a piece. I shook my head.

"Even if I got converted, isn't there a fifty-fifty chance I'd die and stay dead?" I asked. "It's a dangerous operation."

"Oh, we can do better than that," he said. "That statistic is a bit skewed by all the vampires who try to do conversion without knowing what they're doing. They don't exactly teach it down at the Shaker Heights Institute of Technology, you know. You have to learn by trial and error. A vampire who can do it well can almost guarantee you'll come out okay."

"And this sicko friend of yours can do it well?"

"Yeah," he said. "He's a real pro."

Even back when becoming a vampire was a major status symbol a few years back, I never went through that "omigod I wish I could be a vampire and live forever" phase, like a lot of girls.

Having to be seventeen for a full year is bad enough.

If I had to stay this way, I'd just end up all emo and mopey and douchey, like every other teenage vampire. Like, all the dark side that I kept under the surface would probably become all of who I was. There was no way I would end up being some intellectual hippie peace chick. I'd be carrying my crowbar everywhere I went, and I'd be strong enough to do a whole lot of damage with it.

"You don't have to decide right now," said Gregory. "You can take your chances and try to get Fred to go out with you if you want. But you'll never manage it. We both know it. If the dance comes around and you don't think you're getting kissed, I'll be by your car, waiting. I'll have a letter of consent ready for you to sign, and a cigar that'll put you to sleep."

I gave him a dirty look and tried to be brave.

"Go to hell," I said.

"I've been there," he said. "Take my word for it, you do *not* want to be there during tourist season."

He wandered over to the bathroom mirror and started drawing in the fog with his finger—the drawing was either a dog's face or a naked woman; I couldn't tell. But I could certainly guess. He signed it by writing a swear word in the bottom corner.

"It's really very nice of me," he said, "giving you a way to get around the deal. I get paid and all, but it's still very nice of me, don't you think?"

"You're a dick," I said.

"So's your old man," he chuckled.

Everything he had said kept sinking in, until finally I buried my face in my hands and just started to cry. I was facing death, and it was all my fault for being such a terrible person.

When I dared to look up, Gregory was gone.

I sat there and sobbed and thought for a few minutes about all the things I had done wrong.

I was a fraud. A completely ordinary girl who wanted more misery than happiness in the world. More violence than peace.

And now I had to either seduce a vampire or choose between dying and becoming a vampire myself, which meant that I'd be this miserable and pathetic forever.

I wanted to grow up.

I wanted to live my *life*.

After a while, Amber came into the bathroom.

"Jennifer?" she said. "Are you okay?"

I shook my head. "No."

"What's wrong?" she asked. "You seemed so happy a few minutes ago!"

"I'm not sure I can ever be happy again," I told her.

She looked over at the mirror, at the swear words and the drawing of the naked woman, then back at me.

"Did you do that?" she asked.

I shook my head.

"Did Mutual do something wrong?" she asked. "You've got to give him some time, sweetie. He's still new to all this stuff."

"No," I said. "He's been perfect today. It's all me."

"What's the problem?"

"I'm a terrible, terrible person," I said.

"Oh, sweetie!" she said as she gave me a massive hug. "No you're not. You're awesome! Everyone thinks so."

"No," I said. "I'm terrible, and fat."

"You're no fatter than I am. Who cares? You look great!"

"I'm also mean, and rotten, and a big fraud. And now I have to get Fred to kiss me at the dance."

"Okay, back up," she said. "Explain that last part."

I took a deep breath and gave her the short version of the story. The little weirdo who had called me Grimace was some sort of magical pre-human who was using a limited allowance of magic to grant me a few wishes, including having Mutual come to town, but now I had to get Fred to kiss me at the dance, or I'd take my last breath in the high school gym—if I didn't want to become a vampire, so the death wouldn't take. And it was all because I'd wished for Cathy to be miserable.

When I got through the story, Amber's mouth was hanging open as if she were a codfish or something. I was sure, for a second, that she was horrified to find out what a spiteful, awful person I was.

But then she took a step back, looked at the drawing in the mirror again, and turned back to me and started to chuckle.

"You think this is funny?" I asked.

She moved from chuckling into actual guffawing.

"First of all," she said, "you are just about the *least* spiteful and hateful person I've ever met. You've never intentionally harmed anyone or anything, except for some cheap crap from the dollar store."

"And Cathy Marconi's nose."

"That was an accident, sweetie! You felt terrible about it."

"Seriously, though!" I said. "I'm being stalked by a fairy godmofo, and I'm probably going to die! This isn't funny!"

"Yes it is!" she said, between laughs. "That's what's so funny. There're, like, a million girls out there who are saying 'Omigod, I'll just die if I don't get to go to the dance!' But you really mean it."

She laughed some more.

"You don't think I'm awful?" I asked.

"Jennifer," she said, "this is the kind of thing that could *only* happen to *you*. First you almost get kicked out of town over a sixth-grade spelling bee, and now this. You're totally going to survive it, even if this Grue guy isn't just messing with you. We'll all help. It won't even be hard!"

That was when I first cracked a smile. Not a big one or anything, but one corner of my mouth turned up a little.

I really think that if Amber hadn't come in and started laughing, I would have ended up sitting in the corner, rocking back and forth and crying. I probably would have kept doing it until the very night of the dance.

But instead, after a few minutes of talking to her, I stood up, stretched out, did a karate chop in the air, and said, "Well, let's do this thing."

Amber always did make me feel braver.

I wasn't some terrible person who deserved to be miserable, damn it.

I was St. Jennifer the Purple.

And I had the best friends a person could ever want. As long as they were around, I was sure I could handle finding a way to get Fred to kiss me. How hard could it be to get some guy to like me just long enough to kiss me at a dance?

And I could deal with a little weirdo like Gregory Grue. He'd be out of magic and back living in the trees soon enough.

When we came out of the bathroom, the radio was playing the Beatles' version of "Till There Was You." Jason and Mutual were still playing Pac-Man.

"You okay?" asked Jason.

"Jennifer's having a weird night," Amber said. "You want to tell them everything or should I?"

"You do it," I said. Then I leaned over and whispered, "But don't say I wished for Mutual. I'm afraid that might be . . . too forward, you know?"

She nodded, then gave them a very short version. Their

mouths fell open early, but the way Amber told the story made Jason start to giggle before she was halfway finished.

"So, anyway," I said when she was done, "I need to apologize in advance, Mutual. I have to kiss another guy. It's kind of a matter of life and death."

He hadn't said a word through the whole story.

But a smile spread across his face, and then he pumped a fist into the air.

"I love Iowa!" he said. "Something is always *happening* around here."

We all laughed. "Mutual," I said, "you must be the only person in the world who comes to Iowa for excitement."

"I don't know," said Amber. "Someone from Nebraska might have tried it."

Amber hadn't told Mutual that I'd wished for him, but I'm sure it must have occurred to him that it couldn't have been a coincidence that he got a ticket right around the time I'd been offered three wishes.

"Sounds like we've got a mission in front of us," Jason said.

"An epic quest!" said Amber.

Mutual raised a can of grape soda and launched into a spirited excerpt from the St. Crispin's Day speech from *Henry V*, the Shakespeare play he and I had both read in sixth grade.

" 'We few, we happy few, we band of brothers'!" he shouted.

"Hear, hear!" I shouted.

And for a few minutes, we sat around on top of the washing machines and talked strategy, like getting me kissed was going to be a really fun challenge.

Now, once the "Jenny" in Eileen's book gets the

assignment to kiss Fred, she and Amber embark on a whole series of harebrained schemes, like convincing Fred that she's secretly a rock star in disguise (with help from her fairy god-mother, who takes out her wand and makes her look just like Elvis—or what's left of him—every time she takes off her glasses).

Or pretending to be a foreign exchange student.

Or (and this was my favorite) having Amber spread a rumor that every *other* girl in school has the black plague, and Jenny's the only one he *can* kiss if he doesn't want to get it himself (I don't think the plague would *kill* a vampire, but I bet it still isn't the most pleasant disease to have).

Well, we really did consider all of those that night in the coin laundry on Merle Hay. But we were bright enough to know they'd never work.

In between schemes, the Jenny in the book mostly stares out her window and cries. And all that would happen to her if she didn't get kissed is that she wouldn't become the princess of some weird kingdom where they measure ability to govern by one's ability to get kissed (Eileen never says exactly what she's going to be the princess *of*, but my guess is Panama City).

Meanwhile, I had death hanging over my head. *Death*, people. The kind of thing that made Hamlet spend the better part of a six-hour play moping around his castle, acting more emo than a teenage vampire.

And what did my friends and I do?

We laughed our heads off.

We few, we happy few.

Jenny stared out her window, wishing her fairy godmother would float in from the clouds and cast her another spell. She wasn't sure she could ever get Fred to like her without magic to help. She thought about life going on the same old way—with her not being a princess—and a tear began to form in the corner of her eye.

Sometimes, life just seemed harder than she was pretty sure it was supposed to be.

The word echoed in her head all night long: "Princess . . . princess . . . princess . . . princess . . ."

fourteen

Yeah, life's hard, all right. But we were still laughing as we started driving back toward my house.

And you've probably noticed that Gregory had never said a word about making me a princess. But there is a princess in this story. In a way.

"You know what?" said Jason. "I believe your story and all, but I don't really believe you're going to die if you don't get Fred to kiss you."

"Me neither," said Amber. "Gregory is probably full of crap."

"Turning the Weather Beacon purple is probably just a matter of getting enough cellophane over the white bulbs," said Jason.

I nodded. "And it's not like you have to use fairy magic to buy purple paint. Or FedEx a ticket to Alaska, even."

When my car stalled out a few blocks from my house, we

didn't wait for it to start up again. I just put it in neutral, rolled it to the side of the road, then put it in park and ditched it. We started walking back toward my house, taking cheap shots at Gregory and plotting to get me a date with Fred anyway, just for the sheer challenge of it (and, you know, to be on the safe side).

But as we got closer to my house, I started to smell something weird. The odor got stronger the closer we got.

"Wow," said Jason. "I don't want to offend you or anything, but have you been letting the Diarrhea School for Boys use your backyard as a gym or something?"

"Not that I know of," I said.

When we went around to the back of my house, I saw it.

A unicorn was walking around in my backyard.

An actual, living unicorn.

Just like Gregory had promised that night in my car. My knees began to shake, and I felt the hair on the back of my neck stand at attention.

I was past the point of thinking that Gregory was a wild substitute teacher who was trying to reach poor disadvantaged me, but I still hadn't been totally sure about the "magic" aspect of his routine. After all, he hadn't fixed my car, had he? Or gotten me a million dollars?

But this proved it. The second I saw it, I knew that if Fred didn't kiss me at the dance, I was absolutely going to die.

"Oh my God!" said Amber. "It's a unicorn!"

I hadn't told her the part about the unicorn. Not yet.

The unicorn wandered up to the gate and stared at us over it.

Sometimes you see an animal up close and it looks

disgusting, but the unicorn was the most gorgeous thing I'd ever seen. It was majestic, really. Sparkling white, with a beautiful horn.

Stuck on the horn was a note.

Dear Jennifer,

Hoo hoo!
Here's your unicorn, like I told you Friday night.
Believe me now?
Her name is Princess.

She eats the blood of Christian babies, but I already fed her, so she won't need to eat for another month. And don't worry—she'll disappear after Saturday, so you won't have to worry about the cleanup. Or, anyway, your estate won't. Ha ha.

And don't think the fact that you probably won't live until opening night means you shouldn't learn your song for the show!

—G.G.

I read it, then crumpled it up.

"Was that from him?" asked Amber.

"Yeah," I said. "I told him on Friday that if he was for real, I wanted a unicorn as proof. I guess he's real after all."

"Well, don't panic," said Amber. "We can still get you through this."

Maybe it was just a flip side of the violent nature I tried my best not to deal with, but the whole thing about feeling like I had the icy hand of death tapping at my shoulder wasn't really freaking me out, at least not right then.

In fact, it was a rush.

It made me feel more alive than ever.

The unicorn breathed and made a little horse noise. Its breath hung in the cold air, but it wasn't white, like human breath. It was the green color of stink lines in cartoons, which was appropriate enough. The unicorn might have been gorgeous, but it smelled like eleven thousand rotting corpses, all wearing dirty socks, being served flambé with a glass of open butt on the rocks.

And the thing that Jason had said about the gym.

I stepped through the gate, careful not to let it out. It seemed friendly enough, even if it did stink to high heaven.

"Hi," I said. "Your name is Princess, right? I'm Jennifer."

The unicorn actually knelt down on the ground for a second before standing back up.

"This is so cool," said Amber. "I mean, it sucks that you're being stalked by a creepy mofo and all, but I always wanted to see a unicorn!"

There was a leash, or harness, or whatever you call it, hanging off Princess, and I picked it up and led her through the backyard. Jason and Amber and Mutual followed along.

Mom stepped out onto the porch.

"What in God's name is that thing?" she shouted.

"Unicorn," I said, as casually as I could.

"So now unicorns are real, too?" she asked.

"I guess so," I said.

Mom just shrugged as she looked at Princess from across the yard. In a world where we'd found out that vampires, zombies, and all those things were real, the fact that there was such thing as a horse with a horn coming out of its forehead wasn't that big a deal, even for people who *didn't* assume every fantasy creature was real (like you-know-who).

"He sure *smells* real," Mom said, lifting her shirt collar to cover her nose.

"She," I corrected.

"Whatever," she said, through a layer of cotton. "Do you mind telling me what a unicorn is doing in the backyard?"

I thought about telling Mom the whole story, but no good could come of that. She'd just freak out and make it that much harder for me to get kissed by Fred.

"Someone offered me one," I said. "Someone I met at the alliance meeting. I'm babysitting her for a few days."

"And what made you agree to that?"

"What girl would turn down a unicorn?" asked Amber.

"Any girl that had smelled one," Mom said.

She had a point.

"Well, I hadn't smelled her." I said. "How could I turn down the chance to have a unicorn?"

"Very simple," said Mom. "You just say 'No, I don't have any place to keep a live unicorn.'"

"Well, I can't take her back now," I said. "She won't exactly fit in the backseat of my car. But we can put her in the shed."

Mom sighed, then held her nose. "Just a couple of days?"

"No longer," I said. "And I'll take care of her. They only eat once a month, so I don't have to feed her or anything."

"I guess there is probably room in the shed," Mom said, "now that there aren't many tools there. We can use that as a stable."

I grabbed an end of the leash or harness or whatever and led her to the tool shed that Dad built when I was a kid. Inside, there was nothing but a couple of hammers, some shovels, and a box of screws.

"This won't be the most comfortable place to sleep, Princess," I said, turning to her and stroking her beautiful mane. "But it should be warmer than running around the yard. Drier, too."

Princess snorted again, and I heard a fart noise and a plop.

It didn't take a genius to know what had happened, but it took a second for the stench to hit my nose.

When it did, I ran. Literally.

It made my insides scrunch up, like some of the organs inside me were trying to escape up my throat.

I ran out of the shed, shut the door, and raced across the yard. I thought I was going to be sick.

Mutual, Amber, and Jason were already running. I followed them clear down my street, yelling and laughing all the way to my car.

The car started back up, like it normally did after a few minutes, and we drove off, rolling down all the windows and turning the AC to full blast. The smell had come in with us.

"Holy crap!" said Jason. "That is *foul!*"

"There's nothing holy about that crap," said Amber.

Mutual just grinned the whole time. "I love this town," he said.

He was 100 percent alive, all right. And he finally seemed . . . awake.

Maybe it was the fact that we had an epic quest in front of us now that had woken him up, but I reminded myself that he had already been pretty well awake before we got to the coin laundry. If anything woke him up, it was me kissing him.

This was a pretty super thing to reflect on.

We drove through Preston up to Jason's house. When I pulled into the driveway, the headlights hit three people standing there with their arms folded across their chests.

One was Mrs. Smollet.

The other two were Mutual's parents.

When Jenny got near home, she put her glasses back on and felt the strange, tingling sensation that always came when she went from looking like Elvis to looking like herself again. As she pulled into her driveway, she found Mutual and his parents, Norm and Norma Scrivener, standing on her porch.

"There you are," said his mother angrily. "Our Mutual tells us that you are trying to back out of your agreement to give him a kiss!"

Mutual puckered up, and Jenny began to panic. If Mutual kissed her before Fred did, the spell would be broken and she'd never become a princess!

"That agreement wasn't legally binding!" she said. "We were both minors, and it wasn't notarized!"

But Mutual and his parents would not be lawyered.

fifteen

I did, in fact, begin to panic when I pulled into the driveway and saw Mr. and Mrs. Scrivener standing there with Mrs. Smollet. None of them looked happy.

I'd only met Mutual's parents (who really are named Norm and Norma) once before, when he had talked them into taking him to the Breakfast for Supper Banquet, the annual pancake jamboree at the school in Preston to honor the students competing in the district spelling bee. That night, they had come dressed in matching clothes, and acted like they had matching rods up their butts.

They didn't seem much different now. But they did seem angrier.

Mutual swore under his breath.

"We can hear that, son," said Mutual's dad.

The minute I saw the three of them, the first thing that ran through my mind was that there was a vampire out there someplace who was paying Gregory Grue to make girls consent to convert. And these three struck me as suspicious.

I stepped out of the car, determined to ignore them, and walked up to Mrs. Smollet.

"Boy, am I glad to see you, Mrs. Smollet," I said. "I want to talk to you about Mr. Grue."

"I've already spoken with Cathy about him," she said. "I'm sure you can all live with him for half a semester."

"But he's been doing some really inappropriate stuff!" I told her. "He's working for some vampire, too. Don't suppose you know anything about that?"

"He's not important right now," said Mrs. Smollet. "We've come for Mr. Scrivener."

"We always knew you would come back to Iowa for this girl, son," said Mutual's mother. "Even after we explicitly forbade you to leave Alaska. We know your tricks and manners."

"And we found more than one of those postcards you tried to send," said his father.

His mother disappeared and reappeared in front of the car door.

"Come, Mutual," she said. "We are going home."

Mutual sat in the car, looking scared.

"You can't force him to go if he doesn't want to," I said. "He's eighteen."

"You didn't tell me that," said Smollet to Mutual's parents. "We can't take him anywhere against his will if he's eighteen."

"He is still our son," said Mutual's dad.

"But I think your council would frown on you forcing him to go to Alaska with you," I said. "That would be an attack on a human."

"She's right," said Smollet. "Stand down, Norma. If he doesn't want to leave, you'll have to do the diciotto here in Iowa."

Mutual's mom took a step back.

Jason and Amber got out of the car, and the three of us stood next to it, staring at the three of them. I wasn't sure what to do. Challenging them to a fight would have been a waste of time.

"I remember you two," said Mutual's mom to Jason and Amber. "The ones who taught Mutual that listening to rock music was more important than spelling."

Jason snickered. "I'm bad for good," he said. "Wanna see my tattoo?"

Amber slipped her arms around him.

"And you, of course," said Mrs. Scrivener to me. "The one who convinced him to throw his spelling career away."

"You can't touch Mutual," I said.

"It'll be easier for him if he just comes with us," Mrs. Smollet said. "I'm sure the council will grant us permission for a diciotto. If you care for him at all, you won't subject him to one of those."

"Come home, Mutual," his mother said.

I waited for Mutual to shout out the window that he *was* home, but it didn't happen. He curled up into a ball in the seat of my car, as if he were ducking and covering from a nuclear assault.

So I said it for him.

"This is his home," I said. "Iowa."

"The vampire community frowns on offspring who do not convert," said Mrs. Scrivener. "And on their parents."

"So?" I said. "That's a terrible excuse for wrecking his life."

"Keeping him from dying is hardly wrecking his life," said Mrs. Scrivener.

"Look," said Jason, "we all know you can't touch him without it being considered an attack, and as nervous as everyone gets around here about that stuff, I don't think you want to risk it, do you?"

"All we have to do is say we saw you with Wilhelm or someone from his clan six years ago," said Amber. "And they'll harass you to no end."

"And I can have the honor guard out here in a heartbeat," I said.

None of them said anything.

The council had made it clear that they would punish anyone who did anything *like* attacking a human, especially in Des Moines, very severely. They might have been just talking a big game to keep people calm, but they sure sounded serious to me.

"And no one invited you to Jason's house," said Amber, "so I suggest that you get out of here and leave him alone."

"Then I'll put in the request to the council tomorrow," said Mrs. Smollet. "And you can plan on a diciotto next week."

She vanished. Then Mutual's parents did, too.

I opened Mutual's door, and he sat there, crying and shaking.

He had been full of bravado when it looked like I had to get another guy to kiss me or die, but an encounter with his parents had sucked every bit of it out of him.

"I knew they'd find me," he said. "I knew it."

"This was probably the first place they looked," I said. "You didn't exactly try to hide."

He sniffled a bit. "Do you really think you can help me with a diciotto?"

"I can try," I said. "I can definitely try."

He was shaking as he stood up from the car. "Almost nobody doesn't agree to be converted in a diciotto," he said. "Nobody."

"Don't worry, man," said Jason. "Maybe we can even get Fred to help out. He never seems to think anyone should convert, and we need an excuse to talk to him anyway."

"He never does convert any of his girlfriends, does he?" I asked.

"I'm sure he'll at least be willing to meet with you to give you moral support," said Amber. "And that'll give us a chance to hook him up with Jennifer in time for the dance."

"Totally," I said. "See, it's all going to work out perfectly!"

Mutual nodded a bit but didn't seem any less scared.

"You know something else?" I said. "We all still smell terrible."

Jason and Amber started to laugh, and even Mutual cracked a tiny smile before going back to looking like he'd just been run over by a truck.

"I thought I read someplace that unicorns stink," said Amber.

I turned to her. "You knew they were real?"

"They are and they aren't. They've bred a few by crossbreeding horses with vampire blood or something, but they don't do it very often. For obvious reasons."

We all nodded.

"I think I'd better go home and get my shower on," I said. "We all should."

We said our good-byes and I gave Amber a ride home.

"This was one hell of a first date, huh?" she said. "First you kiss in a graveyard, then you find out you have to get some other guy to kiss you or you'll die, then we have to run away from a unicorn, and then you have a stare-down with vampires who want your boyfriend to convert!"

"I don't know why I'm not more scared," I said. "I should be rocking back and forth, tearing at my hair and screaming right about now. I'm going to die if I can't get a vampire to kiss me in a few days, and Mutual's facing a diciotto. But . . . it's kind of a rush, really."

"Well, you know we'll get through it," said Amber. "It's not like talking a guy into kissing you is *that* hard, if you're willing to fight a little dirty. And you don't mind his feelings getting hurt."

"It's just Fred," I said. "I'm not that concerned about his well-being."

Yeah. I said that.

I feel bad about it now, but right then, I really didn't care much about him. He was just another emo vampire to me.

Someone who was 100 percent alive would surely have known better. But I wasn't there yet. That's about all I can say in my defense.

"You think Mutual's dad might be the vampire who pays Gregory for converts?" I asked.

"I doubt it," said Amber. "I'm a bit more concerned that it might be someone from Wilhelm's clan. But if you don't consent, there's nothing to worry about. Those guys can't possibly get past the border, let alone the city limits, without getting jumped."

"Yeah," I said. "Gregory said he'd put me to sleep and drive me out someplace to have the operation done."

"Or it could be some random sicko who has a pretty good con going," said Amber. "If Wilhelm's clan was really up to that kind of crap, they'd have a much easier time doing it on people in some other state."

The rest of the drive back, we made our plans for the next day. First on our list was to get Fred to meet with us, during which time we'd get advice on a diciotto, then try to get him to take me to the dance. It seemed easy enough. Making a complicated plan, like the Jenny in Eileen's book did, wouldn't have been smart—the more complex a plan gets, the more chances there are for something to go wrong.

If Fred didn't seem receptive at first, we'd just do something the Jenny in Eileen's book doesn't seem to have thought of: bribe him.

Mutual and I were both broke, but Amber's parents were pretty well off, and Jason could always pick up more hours at Fat Johnnie's, the pizza place where he worked. I was really touched that they'd do things like that for me.

Of course, what were they supposed to do? Let me die?

When I got back to my house, I took a really, really long shower. I did everything except scour myself with steel wool. And after I was done, I had gotten the smell off just about every part of me except for my hand, which I'd actually used to touch Princess's mane.

I wrapped that up in some gauze, doused it with some of Val's perfume, then headed downstairs.

I wanted to tell my mom I was being stalked by a weirdo

who was apparently magic, but something told me that she would only make things harder for me. She probably wouldn't believe me, and if she did, I didn't see what she could do about it.

After all, in a few days, it would all be over.

In hindsight, I guess I really should have told her. I should have told everyone who would listen. For a straight-A student with a scholarship, I was certainly acting like an idiot.

But realistically, after a day like the one I'd been having, it was hard to think rationally.

When I thought about Mutual's parents, it got me angry again. I even started looking around my room for something breakable, but then I calmed myself down.

No more breaking stuff. That wasn't helping me.

It was just putting me on a path to end up like Dad. Who, when he thought someone else was trying to sabotage me at spelling, blasted rock music into their house and danced around chanting that I was the queen of spelling.

He's doing a lot better now, really. He's worked hard at it.

But I didn't want to end up in that place myself. I needed to find better ways to stay positive.

If Mutual was going to go through all this stuff for me, I was going to be someone better. Someone worth it. For both of us.

And I wasn't going to give Gregory Grue any more reasons to tell me I was an awful, hateful, spiteful person. Not anymore.

When Jenny went to see the costume-fitter to be measured, she was surprised. The costume lady was her fairy godmother!

She felt her face brightening. Just when she was afraid she'd never get that date!

"Just let me take out my wand," her fairy godmother said. "You're not out of this yet!"

sixteen

I don't get why "Jenny" was still surprised to see her god-mother popping up all over the place by then. I mean, I was a bit shocked to see Gregory Grue on the toilet in a ladies' room, where you don't expect to see guys, period, but other than that, if I had flown to Disney World that week, I would have fully expected to see Gregory Grue playing Snow White.

I even half expected him to show up at my door the next morning in a milkman outfit (even though I think those guys were extinct by the time my parents were kids). And when I stopped into Wackford's for a cup of coffee on the way to school, I wouldn't have been surprised to see him wearing one of those aprons behind the counter.

I met up with Jason and Amber by the flagpole before school started on Wednesday morning.

"You ready to do this?" asked Amber.

"Totally," I said. "Let's go pick up a vampire."

Inside, Fred was next to his locker, deflecting the small handful of girls who wanted to take Cathy's place as his significant other. He brushed them all off, cursing a lot as he did.

"There he is," said Amber. "You want us to come with you?"

"Yeah," I said. "Let's say we need him for diciotto help. That'll be the icebreaker."

Amber and Jason nodded, and the three of us bumped fists.

Showtime!

Fred was digging through his backpack, which I noticed didn't actually have any books in it. He came to high school and all, but it wasn't like he did any homework.

"Good morning," I said.

"Hey," he said. "I'm not looking for a girlfriend, so buzz the buzz off."

I've cleaned up everyone's language for this book (except for Mrs. Smollet and Mutual's parents), but Fred's most of all. He was one of those guys who just couldn't form a sentence that didn't use the F-bomb a few times. He practically used it as punctuation.

"We sort of need your help," I said.

He looked up at me. "I'm not converting *anyone*," he said. "I *said* to buzz off."

"It's not that," I said. "It's just the opposite."

"We've got this friend whose parents are vampires," Jason said. "And he just turned eighteen."

Fred swore and shook his head. "Is he converting?"

"We were sort of hoping you could talk to him," said

Amber. "None of us want him to, and we think he'll need help."

Fred sighed, shrugged, and swore a bit more.

"That's pretty much why I'm here," he said. "I mean, I don't do homework, or pay attention, or even show up half the time, but every now and then I can at least talk people out of converting. If you guys want to meet me after school, I'll definitely talk to him."

"Thanks," I said. "He really needs it."

"You know, Fred," said Amber, "we knew you were a good guy."

Fred shrugged. "I try, I guess," he said. "Sometimes."

I hadn't really known that about him, personally. I'd never stopped to think about why he kept coming to high school—I guess I always thought it was just to pick up chicks.

If he really kept coming in order to talk people out of converting, I had been totally wrong about him. I suddenly felt deeply ashamed of myself.

"That's a shame about Cathy going nuts yesterday," Amber went on.

Fred shrugged again. "All the girls who say they want to convert do, sooner or later," he said. "With people like her, the best I can do is drag my feet and string them along until they either get over it or go nuts. Going nuts is still better than going undead."

"Well," Amber said, "you're going to need to find someone else to take to the dance."

Now he chuckled. "No way," he said. "I wouldn't be caught at a dance anymore. If I dance out of step, that damned honor guard will pounce on my ass!"

"But don't you think it would drive Cathy insane if you took Jennifer to the dance?" asked Amber.

Fred looked up at me, then sort of smirked.

"Nah," he said, "I don't want to hurt her or anything, she's a good kid. But meet me back here after school, and I'll talk to your friend, okay?"

He closed his locker and walked away.

"That went well, I thought," said Amber.

"He smirked at me!" I said. "He'd better not have been thinking we were nuts to think he'd go with *me*!"

"Could've been worse," said Amber. "He said he'd meet with us tonight. If it comes down to it, we can just tell him straight up that you'll die if you don't get kissed by him. I'm sure he wouldn't let you die or anything. He seems nice."

She seemed so confident that I didn't get too worried.

Amber was actually much closer to being a screwball-comedy heroine than I felt like I was. Those women were always confident, and sometimes they turned out to be witches (like she was before it got too trendy). And she came up with ideas that seemed perfectly logical to her but never would have occurred to me.

Sometimes I think the ideas I had for the kind of person I wanted to be weren't really based on eccentrics in screwball comedies at all—I was just trying to be more like Amber.

When I got to the auditorium for rehearsal fourth period, Gregory was sitting in one of the seats, continuing his interview with Eileen. She smiled and waved at me, and he flashed me what I can only describe as an evil grin. I gave him a dirty look and walked up to him.

"We need to talk," I called out as I got closer to them.

He told Eileen to pardon the intrusion, then walked down the row of seats with me.

"Hoo hoo, kiddo."

"I need some clarification about this whole thing," I told him.

"Shut up," he said. "We're not discussing that here. You say another word about it, and I'll call you Grimace in front of the whole class!"

I just glared at him. It was all I could think to do.

"Now take your seat," he said, "and don't say another word until I tell you. I can still make this harder on you, girly. Got it?"

I nodded.

"Good. Any progress on getting the Wells Fargo Wagon moved here?"

"No," I said.

"Gosh," he said with a grin. "If only there were some way you could become strong and fast enough to move it here all by yourself!"

I gave him the dirtiest look I possibly could and took a seat at the far back corner of the auditorium, away from everyone else.

When rehearsal got started, he called me up onto the stage.

"All right, ya groundlings," he said as I climbed up. "Part of being an actor is doing things that scare you. Tapping into your darkest, deepest emotions, the parts of yourself that you keep stored away in a place where the lightbulb burned out and it's too dark to see where the switch is anyway. If you've never been so scared you were pretty sure you almost *died*, you'll never be an actor. Jennifer will now demonstrate the power of deep fear. Sing, kiddo."

I looked at him. "What the hell?" I asked.

He grinned again. "Let's hear your song," he said. "Let's hear how being scared out of your wits can influence you as an actor. Right now. Sing."

"I haven't learned it all yet," I told him.

"Just sing what you can," he said. "But sing it out loud and sing it out strong. Let everybody hear you!"

I just stood frozen in place for a second.

"Come on," he said. "Turn and face your audience."

I turned my body toward the seats, where about two dozen other kids were gathered. They were all staring at me.

I wasn't used to that back then. I guess one of the good things that came out of having a book and a movie made about me was that I got over being nervous about that sort of thing.

But I hadn't been on a stage in years—not since Mutual and I lost the district spelling bee. My brain went a bit fuzzy, and everything went quiet—except for the sound of a bell, like the one they rang when you missed a word at a bee, which was probably all in my head.

Then there was a voice that was probably real.

"Go, Jennifer!" someone shouted. Eileen, I'm pretty sure. The one person in the room who thought I was getting a wish granted right then.

"Sing, kiddo!" said Gregory. "Start with the monologue about dirty books, then sing."

I froze, then said, "Dirty books . . . Chaucer . . . Rabelais . . . Balzac . . ."

This was the mayor's wife's big speech—she was accusing Marian the Librarian of lending out dirty books. She'd never read them herself, but the names of the authors *sounded* dirty to her.

She and Mutual's parents would have gotten along great.

"Emphasize the first syllable of Balzac," said Gregory. "Drag it out and let the L sound roll around in your mouth like a couple of cherries that you want to make glisten before you put 'em out on a tray to sell 'em at a market. And say it like you're highly offended by the word itself. Come on. It's an easy laugh."

If I was supposed to be demonstrating that being afraid made you better at acting, I was failing pretty epically.

I started to blush. I was just about to open my mouth when the door opened and Kyle, the office messenger, walked in.

"Jennifer?" he called up at the stage.

Hearing him felt like snapping out of a trance.

"Yes!" I said. "I'm here. Right here. Do they need me in the office?"

"Yeah," said Kyle.

I was already off the stage and halfway down the aisle.

I saw Eileen grinning at me as I ran past her seat in the back row. She was still probably thinking how wonderful it was that Gregory was working so hard to get me out of my shell and making my dream of being an actress—and sounding like I was saying the word "balls" onstage—come true.

Anyone with the intelligence level of a moose would have been able to tell by how I had acted onstage that I did *not* dream of being an actress. But, well . . . you know.

Kyle led me through the hallways right to Mrs. Smollet's

office. She was sitting at her desk, wearing a black dress and looking particularly grim, even for her.

"Good afternoon, Jennifer," she said. "Sit."

I took a seat, and she looked up at Kyle and said, "Leave us."

It was so over the top that I almost laughed.

I decided to try to take control of the situation again.

"I'm glad you called me here," I said. "I really need to talk to you about Mr. Grue."

"Yes, I know. He gave you Cathy's part, and neither of you is happy," she said.

I glared at her and she glared back at me. I considered accusing her of being in league with Gregory again, but if she was, it wasn't like she was going to admit it. She'd just make it worse for me or something. And if she wasn't, but confronted him, *he'd* make it worse.

"I need to speak with you about your boyfriend," Smollet said.

"I don't have a boyfriend," I said.

"Doug's grave is monitored by security cameras," she said. "Especially at times like these, when rumors go around about Wilhelm and his clan. We know what you and Mr. Scrivener have been up to."

I blushed a little.

"And I also know that you were the main reason he came back to town," said Smollet. "But his parents went to Europe to get authorization for a diciotto."

"It'll never work," I said, though I was starting to tremble.

"They always work," she said. "But his parents aren't

entirely confident, either. And according to them, when they've spoken to him about converting in the past, your name came up as a major reason he didn't want to. They think a letter from you telling him to convert could make a lot of difference."

I laughed. "You want *me* to tell him to become a vampire?"

"Yes."

"Never," I said. "Never going to happen, and if you threaten me, I'll have the honor guard on your butt faster than you can ban a book."

She sat back in her chair. "I could make it worth your while," she said. "I wouldn't ask you to do it simply as a favor. You want the valedictorian slot? I can make that happen."

"My dad would be thrilled, but I don't care about that."

"I know you like Shakespeare," she said. "Did you ever get to meet Marlowe?"

"Christopher Marlowe?"

She nodded.

Christopher Marlowe was a friend of Shakespeare's, back in the day. And he'd become a vampire in 1593. When it first came out that he was still around, people in the Shakespeare Club that I went to got all excited because we thought he'd clear up all the mysteries about Shakespeare. But he didn't, really. Whenever he talked about Shakespeare (who Marlowe called Wild Bill), he just started bragging that he'd written half of the plays himself, as well as most of the famous plays, movies, and rock songs that have been written since. No one really took him seriously.

But it would still be cool to meet him.

"I know people who know him," said Smollet. "I can arrange a meeting between the two of you."

I shook my head.

"Then how about a date with Fred?"

I felt all the blood in my body rush to my face so quickly that my lower extremities started to go numb.

"What?" I said.

"I realize that you're attached to Mr. Scrivener," said Smollet. "But I also know what your generation is like. And Cathy told me this morning that you always liked him and wanted to go to the dance with him."

"She's just being paranoid," I said.

I thought about yelling "Nice try, Marconi!" loud enough that she could hear it over in the in-school suspension room, but decided against it.

"He owes me a favor for keeping the council from shredding him along with Wilhelm after the attack three years ago. I can arrange a date. I can probably even keep Mutual from finding out, if you were planning on cheating behind his back like a shameful little girl."

I thought for a second. If she could get me into the dance with Fred, it would be a major step toward staying alive. I *did* need that date.

Maybe I could write a letter to Mutual, then tell him it was all crap ahead of time before it could do any damage.

Smollet must have guessed I was thinking that, because she said, "Of course, we'd have to keep you isolated after writing the letter, so you couldn't try to undermine its effect. But if you were to write a letter right now, we could arrange to set you up at the nicest hotel in town until after the diciotto. We'd let you out to attend the dance with Fred—under guard, of course."

"I don't know," I said as I ran through a list of options in my head.

Could I get around the isolation somehow?

Would Mutual believe the letter in the first place? Under normal circumstances, I was sure he'd see it for a ruse right away, but a diciotto isn't a normal circumstance. No human knows exactly what goes on in one, but it's something like brainwashing. No one can be trusted to think straight during a diciotto.

"Let me think it over," I said.

"No dice," she said. "You could give him a warning. If you leave now, the only way we could use you is if you actually attend the diciotto yourself and tell him to convert."

"Not going to happen," I said.

"Jennifer, the diciotto is happening," she said. "The council *will* grant permission. And it *will* work. His parents have some doubts, but the truth is that without you, it will only take longer and be harder for him. Think of what you're subjecting him to. I saw how he reacted to just seeing his parents last night."

I heard her voice in my head telling me, *"Don't do this to him."* It was an old vampire trick—if they're nearby, they can send their voices into people's heads, where they echo around like, well, like voices in your head. I didn't think it had ever been done to me, but I sure didn't like it.

"Get out of my brain," I said.

"Don't worry," she said. "I can only send my thoughts in, not get yours out."

"Well, knock it off, anyway!" I said. "That's really rude, if you ask me. Can I go now?"

"Just think about how difficult an experience you want to subject Mr. Scrivener to," she said. "And come see me when you change your mind."

Mrs. Smollet's real name wasn't Mrs. Smollet, by the way. It was Mrs. Fartknocker.

I walked out of the office and went into the bathroom for the rest of the period. I wasn't going back to that auditorium for anything.

I wondered, for a minute, if Mrs. Smollet actually had a point—that the diciotto would probably convince Mutual to convert. Just seeing his parents had left him crying the night before. If he converted quickly because I told him to, that was probably better, in the long run, than if he converted because they'd made him feel like he was worthless if he didn't.

I knew a little bit about what it was like to have someone tell you you were awful. And what Gregory Grue was doing to me was probably nothing compared to what would happen in a diciotto. Sparing Mutual that experience would be a humane thing to do.

But I could never betray him like that.

For one thing, I had entirely selfish reasons. If he was going to be my soul mate or whatever, I wanted him to grow old with me, not stay eighteen forever.

And there was hope—his parents, who knew more about diciottos than I did, weren't sure it would be successful without me. Hopefully Fred could teach him a few more tricks that would give him an edge, and I wouldn't need to make such an awful decision.

At the end of the school day, Jason, Amber, and I met up with Fred at his locker, and I heard Mrs. Smollet's voice in my head saying, *"Think it over."*

"Where's the kid?" asked Fred.

"He's not in school," said Jason. "We have to go pick him up at my house."

"Did you drive here?" asked Fred. "I just ran."

"I can drive," I said. "Let's go."

We walked through the parking lot up to my car and I let Fred into the front.

When he took his seat, he stared at the carved wooden dashboard.

"Oh my God," he said. "I know this car."

"You do?" I said.

"Where did you get it?"

"Two hundred and fifty bucks at an auction. But I lost on the deal."

He nodded.

"Do you know whose estate it came from?" he asked.

I shook my head, and he turned to me and said, "This was Doug the Zombie's car."

In the glove compartment of her Prius, Jenny kept a little box containing a lock of hair from a vampire—she felt like it gave her luck. She held it to her chest, hoping it would work some magic on Fred that even her fairy godmother hadn't been able to do.

seventeen

"You're kidding," I said. "This was Doug's?"

Fred nodded sadly.

"Wow," I said.

"It stalled the other night right outside that cemetery where he's buried," said Jason.

"Makes sense," Fred said with a nod. "It knows."

"It stalls all the time, actually," I said.

"You were there that night, weren't you?" asked Amber. "When he and Alley got attacked?"

"It wasn't what people think," he said defensively. "*I* wasn't attacking them. Not really. I honestly thought we were just pulling a prank on them. I even brought Doug some brains from the Science Center to eat so he wouldn't hurt so much while he was crumbling."

"It was mostly Will doing the attacking, right?" I asked.

Fred stared off into space for a while. "It was mostly Will, yeah," he said. "Will was . . . magnetic. He drew me to him, you know? I thought we were just going to, like . . . scare them. Even that would have been cruel, but he could talk me into anything. You ever wonder what you're really capable of, deep down?"

I nodded.

Sincerely.

"I never really felt like I fit in with the other vampires," he said. "But with Wilhelm . . . I felt different. He was smart as hell. Dude had social graces to the nth degree."

"You know, there were some tapes in the glove compartment when I bought the car," I said. "I've never played them. They must be Doug's, though."

Fred opened the compartment and pulled out a cassette, which he popped into the player.

It started playing an old show tune; then that faded out and there was a song with weird lyrics sung by a guy who sounded like he had a cold. Not as gruff as Gregory Grue or anything, but deep and smoky.

"Do you know Alley?" Fred asked me.

"Not that well," I said.

"I talked to her a lot after the whole thing at prom," he said. "This is Leonard Cohen. They were both into him. This is probably a mix tape he made for her."

"Weird," Amber said. "It's like we're listening to someone else's love letter."

"You want to turn it off?" asked Fred. "I kinda think this guy sucks, personally. We could put on some metal or something."

"Nah," I said. "I kinda like this. And the car seems like

it's been running better since you turned it on. I'm hitting the brakes and it doesn't feel like it's about to stall out."

Fred smiled a bit. "It knows."

"Usually it stalls about once a block," I said. "Every trip is an adventure in this machine."

"Remember that time we broke down outside a cow pasture?" Amber said. "There were, like, fifty cows that came up to the gate and just stared at us."

"They could've been a lot more helpful," I said. "Cows don't know *anything* about cars."

Jason and Amber laughed, and Fred gave a tiny grin.

Mutual was on Jason's porch, waiting. He still looked freaked out, and even after we introduced him to Fred and got him into the car, he kept looking over his shoulder, like he was afraid his parents might come climbing out of my trunk any second.

"So, where are we going?" I asked.

"There's a place downtown that only post-humans know about," Fred said. "A place where we can all be ourselves, more or less. And the cops can't get in, so they don't bother to card anyone. I can get you guys in."

"Point the way," I said.

And we rolled off toward downtown, just talking about music, school, and stuff that didn't really have anything to do with post-humans or diciottos or anything. I guess he was building up trust.

Fred wasn't nearly as big a jerk as I'd always thought. He still seemed mopey and unhappy, but that was understandable. I wouldn't want to be a teenager a minute longer than I absolutely have to be. If you've got to live forever, you should do it in, like, your mid-twenties or whenever it is that you hit your prime.

Mutual didn't say a word the whole trip.

Fred directed me past downtown, into the east side, and down a side street into a neighborhood so bad it looked like a set from *Drugs: The Movie*.

I would have been a bit nervous, but it wasn't like anyone was going to mug me or rape me or whatever while Fred was around. They could try, but no gang of toughs could beat a vampire in a fight.

"So, what's this place?" I asked. "One of those new vampire bars?"

"Nah," he said. "This one was a post-human bar even before we came out of the coffin."

"I didn't know there were any of those," I said.

"Sure," he said. "We still keep quiet about it, though, so keep your traps shut."

I followed his directions to a place that looked like a feed store. In fact, it actually said "Feed Store" on the sign, even though I couldn't imagine any farmers living in the neighborhood. The windows were all boarded up, and one of the boards had an Out of Business sign spray-painted on it. The paint on the sign was badly faded and chipped. Weeds sprang up through the cracks in the ground, and even out of the cracks in the paint on the walls.

"Do people from the neighborhood ever try to sneak in?" I asked. "Looks like it would be a nice place for taking drugs."

"They probably try," he said. "But they'd never get past the threshold."

We got out of the car, and Fred walked us around to the

back door and knocked. A little slot in the door opened, and a pair of red eyes looked out at us for a second before letting us inside.

The place looked like any crummy bar I'd seen on TV—dimly lit, with a couple of neon signs, a jukebox, and a pool table. There was a whole lot of sawdust and scattered pieces of rubbish on the bare concrete floor. A tinny speaker overhead was playing an old song with a violin and an accordion. I couldn't tell what song it was, because the lyrics were in German.

It looked like a group of regulars had gotten together to clean up in about 1974, and they hadn't left—or cleaned again—since.

"This is life as a post-human," said Fred. "Dark, dismal, and depressing."

In front of the bar sat three guys, all hunched over. Two of them had their heads down. In the middle sat a much shorter guy. His face was shadowed under a fedora and he didn't turn to look at us, but I assumed it was Gregory Grue. I figured it was best not to try to get his attention.

Just knowing he was there gave me chills, though.

He was *not* going to wreck this for me.

Fred sat down at the edge of the bar, and I sat on a stool next to him.

The bartender gave him a nod.

"What's this, some kind of Nazi music?" Fred asked, tilting his head toward the speaker in the ceiling.

"The Nazis burned this guy's manuscripts in the town square, you dumb punk," said the bartender. "Got some new wannabes?"

"Just one, I think," said Fred.

He ordered a drink, then turned back to us.

"This is the only bar I can get into without a hassle," he said. "I'm actually old enough that most of the kids I grew up with are grandparents now, but as far as most bouncers are concerned, I'm still a teenager. They always think my ID is fake. And, technically, I am still seventeen. My brain hasn't really matured at all since I converted—I'm *just* mature enough to know that I'm stuck being young, dumb, and ugly forever. Believe me, you don't want this."

"I know I don't," said Mutual.

Fred looked a bit surprised. "You don't?"

"Yeah," Mutual said. "I don't *want* to convert. I was hoping for help with getting through a diciotto."

Fred shook his head and swore a little bit.

"Well, this is a new one," he said. "Most of the people I have to talk to are desperate to convert."

"I just want help dealing with my parents," said Mutual.

Fred took a deep breath. "I don't know what to tell you, man," he said. "I've never heard of anyone not converting after a diciotto."

Mutual looked like he was about to cry again.

"Mutual can probably handle it," said Jason. "He's tough."

"No one's *that* tough," Fred said. "I've even seen people pull all kinds of tricks to get out of it, like planting people who don't really want them to convert in the diciotto party, giving them drugs to make them sleep through it, whatever. Nothing works. Nothing. Everyone converts at the end."

I remembered Smollet's offer. "So if I volunteered to help

out at the diciotto, and warned him right now not to listen to me there, it probably wouldn't help?"

"I guarantee you'd just make it worse," said Fred.

"So I'm screwed?" asked Mutual.

Fred inhaled sharply and looked uncomfortable.

"Probably," he said. "I mean, there are exercises you can do to keep them from sending thoughts into your head, which they'll try to do, and that *might* help a little. You know anything about that?"

Mutual shook his head.

"Come on," said Fred. "I can't teach you in here with this accordion racket. Let's go out back."

Mutual nodded and followed Fred out behind the bar, leaving me alone with Jason and Amber—with Gregory Grue still drinking and not acknowledging that I was even there.

"I don't like the sound of this," I said.

"Relax," said Jason. "Mutual can take it."

"I don't know if I *can* relax," I said. "I'm just getting more and more scared about the diciotto, and I don't think I'm any closer to getting Fred to kiss me at homecoming, which means I'm going to freaking *die* on Saturday."

"Not necessarily!" said a growling voice from down the bar.

Gregory, of course.

He hopped down from his barstool and walked over to us.

"Hoo hoo!" he said. "In the dim light of the dusty bulb, purple hair looks black as ebony. You two lovebirds mind if I speak with Miss Van Den Berg alone?"

"Is this him?" asked Amber.

Gregory bowed deeply.

"Rolled into town on Halloween night," he said, "and thought I'd give Iowa a try. I've been helping your friend here reach her full potential."

"And threatening to kill her," said Amber.

Gregory ignored her and motioned for me to follow him. I hopped down from my stool and followed him across the floor, toward the pool table. He stepped to the wall and turned the volume knob next to the light switch, and the German music got loud enough that no one back at the bar could hear us.

He held a pool cue out to me.

"You play?" he asked.

"Never tried," I said.

"It's easy. You hit the cue ball toward the numbered balls and try to get them into a pocket. Any boob can do it."

He set the balls into a triangle, picked up a smaller cue of his own, and shot the white ball toward the triangle, causing the balls to break up. They rolled around all over the table, but none went into a pocket. He grabbed a knife off a table and started using it as a toothpick.

"Your shot," he said.

I found a ball that was sitting right by a pocket, hit the cue ball toward it, and knocked it in. Nothing to it.

"Nice," he said. "Shoot again."

I shot at the nine ball and missed. He took his turn and started sinking ball after ball.

"Now," he said, while he shot at his fourth ball, "why don't you explain to me how you got Fred to take you into a place like this?"

"Because if I tell you, you'll probably just do something to screw it up."

"Smart," he said as he sank another ball. "I certainly will."

He finally missed one, so I took a shot at the four ball, which was purple. It went in, so I took a shot at a red striped ball and missed completely.

Gregory sank three in a row, then reracked the balls.

"I'm going to miss all this," he said. "Saturday at midnight it's back to normal for me. No more messing with humans with magic. We've got it rough, my people. We get one year out of twenty to live in the world, and fifty-one weeks of that I just bum around from job to job like a regular McHobo. Then it's back into the trees to hibernate for nineteen more years."

"So you were never with the RSC," I said.

"Not for three whole years," he growled. "But I do know my Shakespeare. It's hard to stay on top of things when you have to piece history together one year out of twenty at a time. But Shakespeare's been popular the last several times I've been out and about. I saw John Wilkes Booth play Hamlet."

"Did you really?" I asked.

He nodded. "McVicker's Theatre, Chicago. June 28, 1862. Thought he was overrated, myself."

He sank another ball, then paused to rub some chalk on the end of his cue.

"Now, if I overheard correctly, your little boyfriend is facing a diciotto."

"He can take it," I said.

Gregory finally missed a shot and went back to leaning on the cue.

"I've got news for you, kiddo," he said. "No one can take a diciotto. No one. Ever. That boy is going to be a vampire by Thanksgiving—mark my words. If you want to go on being with him, I think you'd better let my vampire friend convert you while you still have a shot at doing it safely. Otherwise, he'll be a vampire hunk and you'll just get older and fatter till you croak."

I sank a ball of my own and took aim at another.

"What does this guy pay you, anyway?" I asked.

"It's more than just money," he said. He put one end of the pool cue on the ground and put his chin on the other, leaning on it like a gnome on his cane. "Far more."

I tilted my head toward the bums at the bar.

"Is it one of those losers?"

"No. Don't worry. Someone more attractive. You won't see him, but I'm sure you'd rather it be someone a little more dashing, right?"

I couldn't help but think he might mean Wilhelm, but I knew that Wilhelm was dead, and for real. I wasn't going to fall into the trap of believing in paranoid suburban myths.

"I'm not going to need him at all," I said. "The two of you are out of luck."

"You're a failure as a human, anyway," Gregory said. "Nothing unusual about you, other than the fact that you can buy a ten-dollar bottle of hair dye down at the drugstore."

"Just shut up, will you?" I said. "I'm not that awful."

"You're a vengeful, spiteful, boring, stupid, ordinary little girl," he said. Every word was like a punch in the face. "At least if you become a vampire, you'll have that going for you."

"I don't need to be dead to be interesting," I said. "I'll get there."

"Heh," he chuckled. "Yeah. You'll be extraordinary, all right. Extraordinarily dull, unless you turn out to be a serial killer or something."

I took another shot and totally missed.

"Maybe if you had a wooden leg," he mused. "You want me to cut your leg off?"

"No thanks."

He started to sing along to the German tune using English words: "Apples and peaches and pump-i-kin pies . . . I's got the razor if you's got the thighs."

I cringed but tried not to look freaked out. I wanted the only points he scored on me to be at pool.

I was not some violent, horrible person. I had my dark side and all, but no more so than any other healthy person, probably. I simply needed to learn to indulge it less, which I figured would get easier if I just stopped having to be seventeen.

And having Mutual to inspire me to be better would help, too.

You almost never get to see what those charming weirdos in screwball comedies were like as teenagers, but I'll bet most of them were just as miserable and stressed out as every other teenager.

"Just think it over," he said when he finished singing. "You can either die a single loser, or live forever with the boy of your dreams. Seems like an easy pick to me! Corner pocket."

He sank the last ball, tossed his cue onto the table, then tipped his hat to the bartender and walked out the door.

I wandered back to my stool and sat down.

"So what's going on?" asked Amber.

"He's trying to convince me to become a vampire myself," I said.

"You want me to chase after him and kick his ass?" asked Jason.

I shook my head. "He'd just make the whole thing worse for me," I said. "We can kick his ass *after* the dance, when his magic has worn off."

"Hell yeah," said Jason. "Even *I'm* bigger than he is."

I imagined riding the unicorn horn-first into him, then burying his body in a pile of unicorn crap.

Fred came back inside with Mutual, and they both looked discouraged. Apparently things hadn't gone well.

"I don't know what to tell you," Fred said to Mutual. "Diciottos aren't easy, and neither is keeping vampires out of your head."

"I'll ask around at the alliance meeting on Friday," I said. "There are some people there who are against diciottos altogether. I'll make some calls tonight."

"Wish I had better news for you guys," said Fred.

Mutual gulped.

I gulped, too.

"My only advice now," said Fred, "is to run like hell. Go someplace where they'll never find you. It'll at least buy you some time, and maybe you can be older when you convert.

Or maybe they'll let you just sign a letter of intent to convert when you turn twenty-five so you won't have to be a teenager forever. I wouldn't wish being a teenage vampire on a flea on the back of my worst enemy's dog."

Mutual fixed his eyes behind the bar and didn't say anything. His lower lip quivered, like he was about to cry.

God, I hated to see him like this.

"Well, where to from here?" I asked.

"Back to school to pick up my car, I guess," said Jason.

Fred settled up with the bartender, we all piled into the Jenmobile, and I drove the five of us away.

"So, Fred," said Amber, "that was weird about Cathy yesterday."

"It wasn't fun," he replied. "You never get used to being dumped, no matter what the circumstances."

"Sounds like she was really bad-mouthing you," said Amber.

"Was she?" asked Fred. "I haven't seen her since Smollet dragged her away."

"So, like we were saying earlier, maybe she needs a wake-up call," said Amber. "What if you took Jennifer, her archrival, to the dance on Saturday?"

Fred laughed, which kind of hurt my feelings.

"But it would teach her a lesson," said Amber.

"And Jennifer's a pretty awesome person," said Jason.

"And it's life or death," I said. "I might actually die. There's a fairy curse going on."

"I've heard that one before," he said. "Look, I thought you guys just wanted me to help with Mutual, not try to con me into taking Jennifer to a dance."

"I mean it," I said. "I'll die of a fairy curse if I don't kiss you at the dance. I am one hundred percent serious."

"She is," said Jason.

Fred sighed. I could tell he was getting uncomfortable. "Forget it," he said. "You can just let me off here."

I started to say something, but as soon as I pulled up to a stop sign he opened the car door and vanished. He was probably already home by the time Jason had moved over from the middle and shut the door.

"Well, that didn't go so well," Jason said.

"Should we go after him?" I asked.

"How could we?" asked Jason. "I don't have a clue where he lives."

"We've still got time to wear him down," said Amber. "We *will* wear him down. We'll bribe him if we have to."

We drove along for a bit, back through downtown. More stuff had been painted purple—the big cow statue outside of the dairy was purple now, too.

Mutual didn't say a word for a long time, but when we made it as far as the west suburbs, he looked over at me. "You . . . you want to be with me, right?"

He looked as nervous as I'd ever seen him (and I'd seen him pretty nervous), but when I nodded, he smiled a little and sat back in the seat.

"I think as long as I remember that," he said, "I can get through it. Just thinking you *might* still want me got me through six years in Alaska. *Knowing* ought to get me through a diciotto. It can't last six years."

I kissed him as soon as I came to a red light, of course.

"But you said you had some friends, right?" asked Mutual. "In the alliance?"

"I'll call them right now," I said.

I pulled over into a 7-Eleven parking lot, gave Murray a call, and asked if he had any advice about diciottos.

Murray groaned. "That's the thing," he said. "The very thing. Diciottos! We've got a whole antidefamation league trying to convince the media that we're safe, normal citizens, but then the council is still authorizing diciottos!"

"Has anyone ever gotten through one without deciding to convert?"

"Probably. People also probably managed to get through being tortured by the Spanish Inquisition without saying that the sun revolved around the Earth. But, you know—not many."

"It's not as bad as the Inquisition, is it?" I asked.

"Actually, as I understand it, it's not that different. They can't physically harm a human in them, but they wear the same red robes that the inquisitors did. And what they do in them things is torture. Psychological torture is still torture."

I ran him through a quick version of the story about Mutual and his parents. He went "hmm" and made cringing sounds in all the right places.

"Well," he said when I finished, "the good news is that the council usually takes a few days to grant a diciotto. They don't consider them to be emergencies, like the request I'd put in to shred any vampire that attacked someone at the dance on Saturday. So he's got a couple of days, at least."

"What about after that?" I asked.

"Best advice I can give this kid is to hide."

"Where could he hide that they won't find him?"

"Oh, nowhere," he said. "But if he stays holed up in your friend's house, at least they won't be able to get him. They were in the driveway the other night, right, not the house?"

"Yeah," I said.

"See? They weren't inside or anything. They won't go into the house if no one invites them."

"Really?" I said. "I always heard those stories that vampires couldn't enter a house uninvited were a myth."

"They are," Murray said. "Those people are thinking of graves, not houses. But going into his house without being invited would be trespassing, and the council won't authorize a diciotto that they have to break a law to carry out. Bad PR. Like diciottos aren't bad enough PR to start with!"

"So he's safe in the house?"

"He could hide there forever. Or until diciottos are outlawed. I give it five, ten years, tops."

"Whatever it takes," I said.

I hung up and relayed the story to everyone in the car.

"I can't just stay in the house forever!" said Mutual.

"We'll be glad to have you," said Jason. "You can stay as long as you want."

Mutual exhaled. "I came to Iowa so I wouldn't have to be locked away someplace anymore," he said.

"Not forever," I said. "Murray said that diciottos will be outlawed in five, ten years tops."

"Five or ten *years*!" said Mutual. "I'm gonna be a prisoner."

"It's worth it," I said. "We're going to get through this. Both of us. Whatever it takes."

Mutual rolled down his window and just watched the streets go by like a condemned man taking a last look at his town on the way to death row.

"Do you want some good news?" I asked him.

"Please," he said.

"Mrs. Smollet said your parents aren't sure the diciotto will work on you."

He turned his head toward me again.

"Seriously?"

"She's trying to get me to help them with it. They don't think it'll work if I don't help."

"Which you know she'd never do," said Amber.

"I thought about agreeing and then showing up to be on your side, but from what everyone's telling me, that'll just make it worse."

He nodded a little.

"Well, that's good," he said. "But did that friend of yours know anyone who got through one before?"

"No," I said. "But he thinks someone must have."

"So, what should I do?" he asked.

"Hide for now, I guess," I said, "at least until we can find something else to do. And if they catch you somehow, just keep in mind that there's hope."

He took a deep breath.

"You sure your parents won't mind me living in your house twenty-four hours a day, Jason?"

"What else are they going to do?" Jason replied. "Throw you to the wolves?"

"I'll have to stay locked away," Mutual said, "and be very careful about opening the door to strangers."

"We'll get you all set up," said Jason. "We'll turn the basement into a whole apartment for you. It'll be great!"

Mutual nodded, exhaled, and said, "Okay. Let's do it."

I drove them to Jason's car, followed them to Jason's place, and watched Mutual walk into the house that would be his prison for the next five or ten years.

Life really sucked right about then.

No one seemed to think Mutual really stood a chance if a diciotto happened. His parents were nervous, but it was probably the kind of nervousness political candidates get the night before an election when they're polling at 65 percent. You can't help but be nervous about something so big.

And it was looking like I might have to become a vampire if I wanted to be up and walking around by the next week.

If I got converted on Saturday, I didn't think Mutual would have a chance at a diciotto, even if I wasn't there. They'd probably convince him that I'd converted just for him, and that he'd be letting me down if he didn't convert, too.

The leaves blew off the trees and onto my windshield so fast that I had to turn my wipers on, and my car—Doug's car—stalled out twice before I turned the tape back on, which really did make it run better.

Maybe being a vampire wouldn't be so bad. I mean, you got to run about a million miles per hour, and lift a hundred times your own weight. There was something to be said for that.

But then I thought about how miserable Fred seemed.

And what a whiny, emo douchebag every other teenage vampire I'd ever known was.

Even the most hard-core Victorians, the ones who really, openly supported diciottos to make vampire offspring convert, never recommended that anyone *else* convert.

I mean, deciding to live forever is a big deal. If I got pregnant or got a deadly STD or got caught robbing a bank or whatever, it could screw up my life big-time, but it would be over in seventy or eighty years. Maybe ninety, if medical science advances a bit and I get enough fiber.

But converting to post-humanism can mess you up *forever*.

I remembered those public service announcements I used to see all the time back when every girl wanted to convert—commercials with girls who had converted and really screwed up their lives (or, you know, their afterlives). They all ended by saying, "Becoming a vampire or zombie isn't just wrong—it's dead wrong."

Gregory's whole thing about how becoming a vampire would suddenly make me the kind of interesting, free-spirited person I had always wanted to be was a flat-out lie.

It would make me into just another mopey, moronic girl.

But it might also be the only way to stay alive.

And my being "alive" might be the only way to keep Mutual alive. Not to flatter myself or anything, but if I dropped dead on Saturday, he'd probably be so upset that he wouldn't be bringing his A-game to the diciotto. Not even close, in fact.

My first instinct when I got home was to break stuff, but I resisted again. After all, it was the night Shakespeare Club met in Cornersville Trace. Shakespeare had always helped me relax.

And, anyway, I was thinking of the old saying that the idle brain is the devil's playground. My mind had been relatively idle all year, which was undoubtedly part of why Gregory Grue was able to mess with me so much.

I needed a Shakespeare Club meeting like zombies need embalming fluid.

Jenny was still desperate to beat Cathy for valedictorian, and she knew that even though it bored her silly, the Shakespeare Club would help her keep her English grades up.

eighteen

That passage of *Born to Be Extraordinary* really hurt.

The Shakespeare Club had always been my favorite extracurricular, partly because it wasn't an official club. The school didn't have anything to do with it. You didn't get any course credit for going, so none of the grade-grubbers from school were ever there. It was just a bunch of people, mostly people far too old to have any grades to worry about, who liked to talk about Shakespeare and met at a bookstore on Cedar Avenue every week to do precisely that.

Mom and Dad had always let me go to the meetings as a special treat back in the day, but it turned out that eight years as a respected member of the Shakespeare Club was one of the best-looking things on my college application. After all, I was planning to major in English for undergrad, and there were people from Drake in the club who were able to put in a few good words for me with admissions.

That night, we were talking about *Twelfth Night,* the play of the month for November—it's one of those Shakespeare comedies that are all about mistaken identity and cross-dressing. Viola, the main character, spends most of the play dressed as a guy. No one at the meeting had ever seen a version where she looked like she actually could have passed, but she somehow managed to fool Orsino, the duke.

They brought out a TV to show a couple of clips from a BBC production where Orsino looked like he'd just wandered in from *The Rocky Horror Picture Show* or something, which was kind of appropriate, since that movie is all about cross-dressing, too.

Really, Shakespeare's comedies are basically the template for those screwball comedies I adore so much.

And while we argued about the finer points of the play, I wracked my brain for a new plan.

When the meeting ended, we all just mingled for a while. As we did, I looked out into the store and saw Cathy Marconi hanging around by the magazines. She was glancing over at me, trying not to look like she was staring. When she caught me looking, she blushed a bit and tilted her head to signal "Come here."

Like I wanted to talk to her.

But I took my cup of coffee from the table where I'd been sitting and wandered over to her. Maybe she'd found a way to get me out of being in the play.

"Hey," I said. "What do you want?"

"I heard you'd be here," she said quietly.

"I never miss Shakespeare Club," I said. "Not since fifth grade."

"Sorry I've been . . . you know," she said. "I know it's not your fault that Mr. Grue is being such a jerk."

"And you knew I wasn't going to slice you from nave to chops with those ice skates?"

She smiled a tiny bit. "Do girls even have naves?"

"Navels," I said. "It means navels."

She nodded. "Well, sorry about that, too," she said. "I was under a lot of stress, and I guess I wasn't dealing with it very well. Maybe I should have just broken some dollar-store junk, huh?"

"Maybe," I said. "If you want a tip, last time I was there they had some great new pieces."

She smiled a bit and flipped through an issue of *Seventeen* that she clearly wasn't actually reading. She looked pretty uncomfortable.

"So, I have a favor to ask," she said.

"Aha!" I said. "That's why you're being nice to me! You want something from me."

She turned a page. "Well, I know I've been totally mean to you lately, and I totally need to apologize for that. But I also need you to go to homecoming with Fred. I'll pay, if you want."

I shook my head back and forth, like I had water in my ear that I needed to get out.

"What?"

"Fred's been saying he won't convert me because I'll end up being just as selfish and dramatic and clingy and whatever else as I am now," she said, with a roll of her eyes. "So I'm trying to show him I'm totally not selfish, and I know that he's not going to be my boyfriend for life or anything, by setting the two of you up."

I looked really hard at her face. She was fake-reading again to keep from making eye contact, so I had to duck down and try to look over the edge of the magazine.

"I overheard Mrs. Smollet saying you were going out with some other guy," said Cathy, "so I'm prepared to pay you. But I need it to be you. It can't be anyone else."

"Why?" I asked.

"Because I've been so mean to you," she said. "And I need to make it up to you. Plus, Fred'll be so impressed that I'm willing to let him go to the dance with my archenemy, he'll *have* to be convinced."

"Archenemy?" I almost laughed. "What are you, nine?"

"You know what I mean," she said.

I took a sip of my coffee and just nodded. I still hadn't exactly forgiven Cathy for her stunt with the skates, and I sure as hell didn't want to do her any favors. But at the same time, the idea that I'd wished for her to be miserable freaked me out so much that I sort of wanted to make nice with her.

And I sure as hell needed that date, even though I didn't believe for a minute that it would convince Fred to convert her.

"What do you want to be a vampire for, anyway?" I asked.

"Well, I don't want to die, for one thing," she said. "Doesn't everyone want to live forever?"

"Not everyone," I said. "It'd get old after a while."

She shrugged. "Don't you ever worry that you're just another boring person from Des Moines?" she asked me. "Don't you want something to make you more . . . interesting?"

I nodded a little.

Let me just say now, kids, that becoming a member of the

undead is *not* the way to become extraordinary. It's the way to become a statistic. But I understood what she meant, all right.

And I needed that date.

"Okay," I said. "But I know he doesn't like going to dances. How are you going to talk him into taking me?"

"Don't worry," she said. "Just leave everything to me. I know exactly what to say to him."

From the look she gave me, I got the idea that she was going to make what Mrs. Shinn, the character either she or I was supposed to be playing, would call "brazen overtures." Like, she'd impress him with her selflessness by suggesting he take me to the dance, and then promise him that I'd do all sorts of . . . unsavory . . . things to him to seal the deal.

I was not quite comfortable with this, but it was a better way to get a date with him than agreeing to be a helper at Mutual's diciotto. And all I had to do was get that kiss. I didn't have to let him go one step farther, even if he wanted to.

Of course, I found out later that wasn't what Cathy told him at all. I had no idea at the time, but I might as well tell you up front that she did something entirely different to convince him to take me to the dance.

It was always her habit to make things *way* more complicated than they needed to be—like planning to stay up for three days to look tired and frumpy onstage instead of just acting.

Or becoming a vampire in order to be interesting.

I've never found out *all* the details of what she told him that night. Whenever I talk to someone who knows, they just blush and change the subject. But what I do know is that she told him I had some gross, embarrassing disease. The kind that involves tumors, discharges, scabbing, twitching, and assorted other unpleasant, highly personal things.

Like, sometimes when you go to the drugstore you see some medical devices that make you say, "Man, I'd hate to have to go to the counter with one of those! How embarrassing!"

Well, from what I've figured out, the disease she told Fred I had required me to use most of them. The closest I've come to finding out *exactly* was when someone who knew told me I was on the right track when I suggested "exploding butt cancer."

I *do* know that she told him it was a miracle I was even still alive, and that what I had to do to stay alive would have killed most people by my age, and that I might not make it much longer. She told him she had found out about it by overhearing the school nurse talk while she was in suspension for throwing a textbook at him.

And that it had always been my dream to be kissed by a vampire.

When Jenny got into her Prius, there was a note taped to the steering wheel from her fairy godmother.

"I have cast you one last spell," she said. "One last chance for you to make Fred fall in love with you. When you smile at him, he will be totally enchanted with you. And when you talk to him, he will find you totally fascinating. The spell should last long enough for you to get him interested. The rest is up to you! Good luck!"

Jenny wiped her eyes, which were still wet with tears. She had thought that her fairy godmother was all out of magic!

She gripped her steering wheel tightly. This was not over yet!

nineteen

Spoiler alert: it wasn't really magic that got "Jenny" her date. None of the spells helped at all. Smiling and talking to Fred and seeming confident about herself were all she'd really needed to do all along.

I couldn't believe girls didn't see that one coming until I started hearing some of them say things like "I never liked reading until I read *Born to Be Extraordinary!*"

That explained it. They didn't see the ending coming because they'd never read a book before!

I guess the master stroke on Eileen's part, the move that made the book a huge hit instead of just another bad book that no one read, was saying that *Born to Be Extraordinary* was a true story and sort of implying that I could make other girls princesses, too. I've learned that some girls would happily read any piece-of-crap book a million times if it made them believe they could be a princess.

I'm only half kidding when I call you kids a bunch of monarchists.

But I did end up finding out that having confidence helped me a *lot*. Certainly a lot more than anything Gregory did.

And there *was* a note from my "fairy godparent" taped to my steering wheel the next morning (along with his favorite swear word scribbled over and over on the windows). But it wasn't exactly an encouraging note.

> *Hoo hoo!*
> *No luck yet with Freddie?*
> *Never fear!*
> *You'll love being a vampire!*
> *Why not convince Mutual to be one, too?*
> *Then you can live happily ever after*
> *until you screw up and get yourselves*
> *torn to shreds!*

I used the cigarette lighter in my car to set fire to the note and stamped it out in the driveway. And I imagined doing the same thing to Gregory, of course.

I wasn't going to die. Cathy was going to talk Fred into taking me to the dance. She might have to make a lot of promises to him that I wasn't about to deliver on, but that morning, I sort of felt like Cathy was the *real* fairy godmother in my story. She had shown up to save the day just when I was so desperate I was coming up with incredibly stupid plans.

And in between first and second periods, Fred came up to my locker, looking a bit nervous.

This was it. Showtime.

Even though I had no plans to follow through on anything Cathy might have told Fred I'd be willing to do beyond kissing, I gave him my very sexiest look.

Of course, I now realize that I probably looked like I had a twitch or something, and Fred probably thought it was just one of the symptoms of my disease.

"Hi," he said.

"Hey," I said.

"Sorry that I disappeared last night," he said. "How's your friend?"

"He's gone into hiding," I said. "He's going to hide out in Jason's house until diciottos are outlawed."

"That might work," he said. "I hear it'll be five, ten years, tops."

All around us, everyone went about their normal routine, digging through lockers and stuff, but I noticed a *lot* of people wearing crosses, and I thought I detected a smell of garlic in the air. The closer we got to the dance, the more paranoid people were becoming about Will and his clan.

"But anyway," he said, "Cathy came by and talked to me last night. She said you two hung out at the Shakespeare Club?"

"Yeah," I said. "We sort of called a truce."

"I'm glad to hear it," he said. "She . . . told me a few things that sort of surprised me."

I saw his eyes go down my body. I blushed about a million different shades of red, because I assumed he was checking me out. What he was really doing was checking whether he could actually see the tumors through my clothes, like she'd told him.

"Yeah," I said. "It, uh, turns out she knew some things I didn't know she knew about me."

"Yeah," he said. "She said she overheard the nurse saying some pretty serious stuff."

I blushed. I guessed she had told him she heard the nurse talk about me asking about birth control or something.

"Yeah," I said. "It's kind of embarrassing to have people know that about me, but . . . you know. All true."

"I mean, she told me you were . . . well . . . I don't know how you survive!"

I blushed a bit more now. I guessed Cathy must have told him I'd somehow found a way to do more than other girls could do with him without getting hurt or killed.

There isn't much vampire guys can do with human girls beyond kissing that won't kill the girl. To start with, they're *really* strong, and in the heat of the moment, they can't always control themselves. I'm sure you all remember the PSA with that girl who lost a butt cheek.

Fred gave me a nervous sort of smile, and I gave him a wink, which he probably thought was another twitch, and he quickly looked me up and down again. I felt like I was a piece of meat at a butcher shop. It was not a way I was used to being checked out. I decided on the spot that I could live with my weight if it kept more guys from looking at me like this.

For the most part, though, I thought he was being a gentleman. He wasn't coming right out and *asking* what it was that I could do with him. He spoke slowly, like he was being careful not to say the wrong thing and seem like he was being too forward.

Of course, he was *really* being careful not to say anything that might embarrass me or make me think he was only interested out of pity.

This is the most humiliating of all the parts of the story for me to talk about, by the way.

"So anyway," he said, "she told me she thought I should take you to the dance on Saturday."

"I know you don't like dances much," I said.

"No," he said, "but she really convinced me that we could have a good time. And I do like you, you know. I think all that stuff you're doing to help your friend is really . . . admirable. And brave. You're totally brave. I like that."

I smiled. "So, you want to go to the dance?"

"If you think you're up to it."

"I'd like that."

"You'll have to drive," he said. "Unless you want to ride on my back."

He was probably just being practical here, but it sounded a bit too forward to me. I did my best to play hard-to-get rather than turn him down.

"I don't ride backs on the very first date," I said in my flirtiest voice. "What do you think I am, some kind of hussy?"

He smiled. "I'll be at your house at seven on Saturday," he said. "See you then!"

And I smiled and walked away.

I had done it.

I *thought* I had just pulled off the greatest acting gig since Viola fooled Orsino.

I was a little embarrassed and all, but the embarrassment and general humiliation were totally overshadowed by the pure elation of knowing I'd pulled it off and I was going to survive the weekend.

By the time I got to rehearsal in fourth period, I was practically dancing my way into the auditorium. In fact, I *did* dance my way in. I was shaking my hips and pumping my fists, doing high kicks and spinning around. *Real* dancing. Self-expression. The kind Audrey Hepburn's character does in *Funny Face*, the movie where she plays just the kind of artsy bohemian I wanted to be.

Eileen was in the theater, taking notes and following Gregory around like a puppy as usual. Her face lit up when she saw me and my sweet moves.

"Well, look at you!" she said. "A week ago you were quiet, shy, and awkward, and now you're almost walking on air!"

I didn't say anything. I just danced some more.

"He does great work, doesn't he?" said Eileen. "You're so lucky to have a fairy godparent!"

"Hoo hoo!" said Gregory from the stage. "What are you so happy about, kiddo? Don't you know that if you're happy today, you'll be sorry tomorrow?"

He seemed genuinely annoyed—which was totally lost on Eileen.

Life felt good.

Not *because* of my fairy godmother, but *in spite* of him.

I danced my way to a seat behind Cathy.

"Guess it went well?" she asked.

I smiled and nodded. "I don't know what you told him," I said, "but he sure seemed eager to take me to the dance."

"Just promise you'll have a good time," she said. "And let's keep the whole thing about you and your boyfriend a secret, okay? Definitely don't tell him I knew you weren't, like, actually trying to steal him."

"Deal," I said.

This was perfect. It would solve the whole problem, and it wouldn't even make Cathy miserable. Gregory was totally failing.

When the rehearsal got under way, Gregory called me up to the stage and told me to pick up where I'd left off the day before, accusing Marian the Librarian of loaning out dirty books.

This time, my head didn't get fuzzy when I stood on the stage. I didn't hear ghostly bells ringing out to say I'd missed a spelling bee word, or feel any flash of fear that anyone was going to put a For Sale sign in my yard if I messed up.

After all, as far as I knew, I'd just pulled off an acting job that took *way* more skill than some school musical.

"Chaucer!" I said, like it was a dirty word. "Rabelais! Baallllllllzac!"

I spit them all out the way Mrs. Smollet would have said the names of deviant sex acts. I played up the first syllable in "Balzac" like crazy, then paused for a moment before finishing the word.

And when I looked out into the auditorium, I saw that people were laughing.

For a split second I thought they were laughing *at* me, but then I realized they were laughing because I was doing a good job of being funny. Even Cathy cracked a smile.

"Now sing!" Gregory shouted.

And I started to sing my part of "Pick-a-Little, Talk-a-Little," and, mysteriously, I nailed it. I was probably pitchy as hell, but I sang it like I meant it, and it worked. I ran around the stage doing the hand motions and all the exaggerated poses the mayor's wife is always doing.

And I actually had *fun*.

But it isn't over for Jenny once she gets that date with Fred in *Born to Be Extraordinary*. She still has to deal with Mutual and his parents trying every dirty trick in the book to keep her from making it to the dance in the first place. And saving Fred from that rebel group that tries to kidnap him.

And the story wasn't over for me, either. Not by a long shot.

After the rehearsal, I glided out of the auditorium. Eileen followed me, notebook in hand.

"That was wonderful!" she said. "You were born to play that part!"

I smiled. "I like this acting stuff more than I thought."

Then, all of a sudden, the tornado siren went off.

In case you're in California or something and they don't have these things where you are, here in Iowa we have alarms that go off in the school when there's a tornado warning, just like the alarms that go off when there's a fire. And a couple of times a year, we have tornado drills.

When there's a tornado and you're at home, you go to the basement. But if one hits and you're at school, the thing to do is duck and cover: get down on your knees, bend over, and cover your head with your hands. Honestly, I don't think hiding from a tornado like that is any better than hiding from a nuclear attack in the same position, but, well, school boards have to tell students to do *something* or people will say they don't care about the students' safety.

All over the halls, people started to get down against the wall, but no one panicked or anything. People who were combing their hair or whatever finished what they were doing first. No one thought it was an actual tornado—everyone knew that we rarely get those in November. But if you don't participate in a tornado drill, you can get detention.

I was just ducking down myself when I saw Murray appear at the end of the hall.

"What the hell's happening?" I shouted at him.

"Get down!" he shouted back.

I got down.

For the next couple of minutes, while the siren next to the school blared, I could hear people running around and shouting.

I couldn't see what was going on, but if Murray was here, obviously the vampire honor guard had been called in. This was no tornado drill.

Then I heard Mrs. Smollet saying, "False alarm."

"We're taking every threat seriously," said Murray.

"Well, this was a false alarm."

The sirens stopped blaring, and Smollet yelled out, "Back to class, everyone. Nothing happened. Nothing to worry about."

I got up and walked over to Murray.

"What just happened?" I asked.

"Someone called in a Wilhelm sighting," he told me. "I figured it was fake, but it was a good drill for us. We were pretty tight, huh?"

"I wouldn't want to be a vampire attacking this place," I said.

He smiled proudly and patted one of the other vampires, a guy with a mustache and a flannel shirt, on the back. "Nice work, Vlad," he said. "You ever meet Jennifer Van Den Berg? She's in the alliance."

"Nice to meet you," Vlad said.

"Hi," I said.

"How's that friend of yours?" Murray asked.

"He's gone into hiding, like you suggested."

"She's got this friend whose parents are vampires," Murray explained to Vlad. "They want to do a diciotto, and I figure his best shot is just staying someplace they'd have to break into until we get those outlawed."

"Five, ten years, tops," said Vlad. "I know that seems like a while to you, but it doesn't seem like too much when you're immortal."

"And hey," said Murray, "nowadays you can go to college online, get your laundry sent out, whatever. No reason to get off your couch, anyway, am I right?"

"Sure," I said. "He'll be fine."

A couple of hours later, I met up with Jason and Amber in the parking lot and told them I'd gotten the date, and that Cathy had actually helped.

"Marconi?" said Amber. "And you don't think she's just setting you up to embarrass you?"

"She might be," I said. "But she got me the date, so I don't care what she's planning to do."

"So what *did* she do?" Amber asked. "Not that I'm surprised you could do it or anything, but I want to know!"

I blushed a bit more, then told them the story.

The three of us looked at one another, then Jason and

Amber started laughing. I actually felt a bit bad for Cathy—she was going to all this trouble, and saving my butt, and I was sure that Fred was never going to convert her.

When we got to Jason's house, we found Mutual pacing back and forth, looking scatterbrained and manic, like this was prison and he'd been in the hole for twelve hours—not just hanging around while we were all in school.

"I have an idea," he said.

"What?" I asked.

"Gorilla suit," he said.

"Gorilla suit?"

"I'll get a gorilla suit. And I'll just wear that every time I go out, so they won't know it's me."

Amber shook her head. "Sweetie," she said, "I think they'll guess that something weird is going on if they see a guy in a gorilla suit coming out of the house."

Mutual made a sort of half-scream, half-grunt noise. The kind of noise you make after you stand in line for three hours and find out they don't have the form you need to sign, then you stub your toe as you're walking out the door.

"It hasn't even been twenty-four hours, and I'm going crazy!" he said. "It's like they're still keeping me locked down. Only now I'm letting them!"

"Maybe we can get you moved someplace else," I said. "I saw the vampire honor guard in action today—I'm sure they could move you to a place of your own."

I had been fantasizing about this all day, actually.

Once I had some money, the four of us could rent a little cottage together in the South of Grand area, or maybe one of those Craftsman-style houses in the neighborhood near the Playhouse, and paint the walls all sorts of funky colors. There would be a view of the city skyline from the roof, where we would have picnics. Life would be great, even if he could never leave.

But he wasn't thinking that far ahead. He kicked the ground a couple more times.

"And I don't even want to think about what might happen if you don't get that date with Fred," he went on. "I should be out there, helping you!"

"Oh, I got that, actually," I said.

He stopped kicking and looked up.

"You did?"

"Yeah," I said. "Cathy thought that if she set him up with me, he'd decide to convert her. It'll never work, but I got a date out of it."

"But I thought he hated dances."

I smiled. "Well, I think she promised him I'd do a lot more than just kissing."

"Okay," said Mutual. "But . . . you won't, right?"

"She couldn't if she wanted to," said Amber. "You probably never saw all the commercials, since you didn't have a TV up there, but this one girl let a vampire squeeze her butt, and it bruised so badly they had to amputate!"

"Is *that* how it happened?" asked Jason. "I always imagined him just squeezing it right off."

"Ew!" said Amber, though she was laughing.

"I wouldn't let him do anything even if I could," I said. "As soon as I get that kiss, I'll thank him for a wonderful evening and be on my way."

And I gave Mutual a kiss, but his face didn't light up this time.

"It's actually kind of mean," said Jason. "Getting his hopes up like that. Poor guy's been a high school horn-dog who can't get any action without killing the girl for decades now."

"He'll understand when I explain it was life or death," I said. "I just hope I don't screw it up. Should I get something . . . enticing to wear?"

"Try not to see him at all between now and then," said Amber. "Not that you couldn't entice him, but now that you've got the date, don't give him a chance to change his mind."

I nodded. "Good point."

We talked over my options, and in the end I decided to skip school altogether—the less I saw of Fred, Cathy, Smollet, and Gregory Grue, the better. I sent Fred a text saying I wasn't feeling very well, so I'd be staying home the next day to make sure I was feeling strong enough to make it to the dance on Saturday.

I didn't realize it, but I had just confirmed the stories he'd heard about my health.

He immediately sent one back telling me to "be strong and do what you need to do!"

Meanwhile, Mutual stared up at the ceiling. After a couple of minutes he stepped away from the conversation and flopped down on the couch. The rest of the evening, when he talked at all it was just low muttering again, like his first night in town, only even weaker. He was back to being broken.

Of course, now that I look back, I shouldn't have been so smug and happy, either. I was so blinded by my delusion that I'd pulled off an impossible scheme that I wasn't thinking about the things I should have been thinking about.

Like the fact that I still had a unicorn stinking up my toolshed that I was too afraid to check on.

And I probably should have been more worried about this "vampire friend" of Gregory's, and whether it was a clue that Wilhelm or his clan was really up to no good.

I should have been wary of what Cathy's real motives were. The fact that she *wanted* me to go to the dance with Fred was super-suspicious.

And I should have known that with forty-eight hours to go until the dance, there was no *way* that Gregory wouldn't be looking for a way to screw things up.

Jenny, you were born to be extraordinary.

—Eileen

Some are born great, some achieve greatness and some have greatness thrust upon 'em.

—Shakespeare

twenty

I don't usually like to disagree with Shakespeare, but I'm not really disagreeing with *him* if I say no one is born great. I'm just disagreeing with Malvolio, the character in *Twelfth Night* who said that. And Malvolio is sort of a dork.

I don't believe anyone is born great, or born extraordinary. Well, Shakespeare was, maybe, and I guess I can think of a couple of other artists and stuff who just seemed to be channeling something divine instead of living their own life sometimes, but that's about it. The rest of us have to work for it.

And sometimes even working for it isn't enough. You really do have to have it thrust upon you to get you started.

That's pretty much what happened to me. If your life gets extraordinary enough, you might end up with no choice but to start being an extraordinary person.

Friday morning, I told Mom I had a headache and didn't want to go to school. I had never faked sick before, so she didn't doubt me.

Just to make sure my date for the next night was still on, I sent Fred a text saying I couldn't wait for the dance.

He sent back a smiley face, so I figured I was okay for the day. I spent the morning on the Internet, trying to see if anyone else had ever survived the threat of death by way of a fairy godparent.

By noon, I think I had read every decent webpage about fairies and known species of post-humans, both living and extinct, in the world, and hadn't found anything that would explain Gregory Grue. He must have been part of one of the "uncontacted tribes" that were known to exist here and there.

If they only came out one year out of every twenty, it made sense that we wouldn't know much about them. They hadn't been in the world at all since the other post-humans went public.

I still had Melinda's piano lesson to teach that day and couldn't really afford to cancel it, so in the early afternoon I forced myself away from the computer and sat down at the piano to refresh my memory on the piece she was working on. I was just about done when I heard a knock.

I looked up to see Mrs. Smollet's face.

"What do you want?" I asked, through the window. "You're not invited here."

"I hate to interrupt your attempt to play hooky," she said.

"I'm playing piano, not hooky," I said in my best smart-aleck voice.

"I needed to confirm that you're still alive," she said.

"Well, obviously I am."

"I can see that," she said. "But there's a rumor going around school that you were killed by Wilhelm's clan this morning."

Now I stood up.

"What?" I asked.

"I know it's nonsense," she said. "But I was sent to check on you."

"Well, here I am," I said. "You can leave now."

I went back to playing piano, but she didn't leave.

"Can I come in?" she called through the window.

"You can see I'm alive," I said. "What else do you need?"

"Please?"

I sighed and opened the window so that she could hear better. I wouldn't have let her into my house for anything.

"I spoke to Christopher Marlowe," she told me. "Or to his assistant, at least. I think I could arrange for you to meet him. You could hear some first-hand stories about Mr. Shakespeare."

"And all I have to do is convince a friend to become a teenage member of the walking undead," I said. "Some bargain."

She looked a bit uncomfortable.

"Jennifer," she said, "I don't much care for diciottos, myself. But I know that his parents are determined to hold one, and I believe the best thing I can do is find a way to make it a quick and relatively painless one for him. You're the key to that."

"The best thing you can do is stop them altogether," I said.

"They'll do this with or without you and me, Jennifer," she said. "Think about what you're putting him through. If you don't convince him to convert quickly, they'll put him through psychological torment you can't even imagine."

I turned away from her and went back to playing, trying to pick out the *Twilight Zone* music just to bug her. When I turned back to look at her again, she had disappeared.

There wasn't going to be any diciotto. Not if I could help it. We'd keep Mutual in hiding until his parents couldn't even think about doing it without getting killed by the council.

I assumed that Smollet was just lying about the rumors as an excuse to bug me about Mutual, but when I went upstairs to my nightstand, where I had left my phone, I found that I had about fifty texts from Jason and probably a hundred texts and missed calls from Amber.

Something weird was going on, all right. Amber and Jason knew I was staying home—they shouldn't have had any reason to believe I was dead because I wasn't in school.

I called Amber, even though she would have been in class, and she picked up.

"What's going on?" I asked her.

"Oh, thank God you're alive!" she said. "When your number called, I was afraid it would be your mom using your phone!" Then I heard her shout out "It's her! She's alive!" and heard the sound of people cheering.

It's kind of nice to hear people cheer that you're alive. Just saying.

"What the hell is going on?" I asked.

"When you didn't show up to class, people started saying Wilhelm had killed you."

"He's busy being dead," I said. "And if his clan comes to town, the honor guard will tear them new ones."

"Well, thank God!" she said. "I didn't believe that you were dead, but it was hard not to wonder, with everything else that happened today."

"What *did* happen?"

"Cathy got converted," Amber said. "She's a vampire now, once she wakes up from the coma."

This wasn't as bad as it sounded. It's actually a very good sign if you're in a coma after being converted. The people who don't survive the operation usually just plain die right away—they don't get as far as being in a coma.

Still. She had been converted. At school, even!

"Oh my God!" I said.

"I know!" she said. "They found her in a bathroom stall, slumped on the floor. Do you believe it? She got converted in the *bathroom*! Ew!"

"So who did it to her?"

"We don't know," she said. "No one knows anything. Most people are saying it was Fred."

"No way," I said. "Why would Fred have converted Cathy? He was totally against that."

"Well, I'm keeping that quiet," she whispered. "If it wasn't him, people will think it was Will's clan or something and they'll go nuts. But as far as I can guess, it's either them, or that plan of hers to impress Fred with her selflessness actually worked!"

"There's no way that worked," I said. "It had to be Will's clan. Is the honor guard there?"

"Some of them are. A few got sent to Canada to check on the clan, though."

"Let me get Fred on the phone," I said. "I'll get to the bottom of this."

I felt myself starting to shake again.

This threw everything right back into chaos.

I sent a couple of texts to Fred, but he didn't reply. There was no answer when I tried to call him.

I put on the TV news, but there was no mention of anything going on yet—whatever was happening wasn't enough of a story to hit the cable news channels. I couldn't even find anything about it online, except for a couple of status updates from people in school who were updating all their pages and stuff from their phones. They didn't seem to know anything Amber hadn't told me.

But I left the news on all through Melinda's piano lesson, and tried to text Fred about every thirty seconds.

Then, while I tried to eat a frozen pizza for dinner, there was a story on the local news about a conversion in a local school. There was speculation that this all had to do with both the dance and the stuff in town being painted purple on Tuesday, but authorities were dismissing it, and the school said the dance would still go on the next night.

As I drove out to the weekly Human/Post-Human Alliance meeting, I tried to get Fred on the phone at every stop sign. There was still no answer.

When I got to the armory, the whole place was a madhouse. Everyone was running around like crazy, and there were actually news cameras, which we normally never had.

Dave, the chairman, was onstage shouting for order.

"We'll cover everything today," he said. "And I can assure everyone that there's no undue cause for alarm! There have been no attacks on humans. The conversion was consensual. Everyone, please sit down!"

Vlad tapped Murray on the shoulder, and the two of them stepped away from me to discuss something as everyone took their seats.

"Okay," said Dave. "I'm going to bring up Principal Ward Jablonski of Cornersville Trace High School to talk about the conversion that took place at his school today, then we'll deal with everything else, okay?"

There was polite applause as Jablonski came onstage. The news cameras got right up in his face.

Corey came over and put a hand on my shoulder, and I just sort of shook him off.

"Not today," I said.

I couldn't figure out why everyone was acting nuts. Conversions in schools had happened before. This wasn't anything new. Something else—something very wrong—was happening. Just when I needed things to go right.

"As far as we're concerned, there was no *incident*, per se, today," Jablonski said, though he seemed pretty nervous to me. "Cathy Marconi had signed a letter of intent months ago. She also signed a letter of consent today, she was of legal age, and there was no sign of struggle. The main issue for us was that, uh, what went on in that bathroom was"—he paused and chuckled awkwardly a bit—"was way over the line in terms of appropriate behavior in a school. Obviously, the vampire who performed the operation shouldn't have been in the girls' bathroom."

People giggled a little, but I could tell they were all nervous.

"Now, the young lady had actually been spending the day in in-school suspension for having attacked a vampire herself," he went on. "The secretary said Miss Marconi had seemed terribly agitated for some reason, and at lunch she begged for permission to be excused to use the bathroom, and, well, she never came back."

I raised my hand but didn't wait to be called on. "Do you think it was Fred who converted her?" I asked.

"Well, we assume so," said Mr. Jablonski. "He wasn't known to be in school today, but . . . Next question, please."

"What if it was Wilhelm's clan?" someone shouted. "Why aren't you canceling the dance?"

"We've sent guard members to Canada to keep that clan under conrol," said Jablonski. "But even if they were involved, if we don't have the dance, we're just letting them win."

"Where's Fred now?" I asked. "What's he saying?"

Jablonski turned pale.

"I'm going to turn things over to the chairman," he said. "No further questions, please."

And he ducked off the stage.

Dave came back up and said, "So you see, folks, no human need be concerned."

"And anyone comes near that dance who doesn't have two forms of student ID, *pow!*" Murray shouted out from the corner, where he was still talking to Vlad.

I walked over to where Murray was.

"What's going on?" I asked. "Something else happened, didn't it?"

"Hey," he said, "don't worry. You saw us in action. No one's gonna mess with you tomorrow night on our watch!"

"But what happened? Why did he dodge my question about Fred?"

Murray breathed in deeply.

"Well," he said, "we need to keep things quiet, otherwise people will panic. There was a vampire-on-vampire attack today, too."

"What?"

"Not a vampire-on-*human* attack," he said, "so you got nothing to worry about."

"Who was attacked?" I asked. "Was it Fred?"

Murray nodded. "If that girl hadn't been converted and the school hadn't sent us out to his apartment, we wouldn't even know about it. But someone attacked him. Probably someone who didn't approve of him converting that girl."

"Fred would never have done that," I said. "It can't have been him."

"Well, I don't have any word from the guys who went to Canada yet," said Murray. "But we've got a pretty good sense of smell—once we get a whiff of those guys, we'll know if one of them was in Fred's apartment. So we've got things under control. No one needs to be worried. Just don't tell anyone, or they'll freak out. That school of yours smells enough like garlic already!"

It had to be Will's clan that had done it. There was no other good explanation for what had happened. One of them had offered to convert Cathy, like she always wanted, and another had taken revenge on Fred for not getting shredded right along with Will.

"Is Fred going to be okay?" I asked. "Like, by tomorrow night?"

Murray turned terribly pale.

"Jesus, kid," he said. "I don't know what to tell you . . . it was a vampire attack. When a vampire attacks another vampire, they don't just knock 'em upside the head, you know?"

"What happened?" I asked. "Tell me!"

Murray took a deep breath. "He's dead, Jennifer," he said. "Whoever it was killed him."

Jenny felt terrified. Fred had been kid-napped! How would she ever get kissed by midnight now?

twenty-one

I took off running away from the meeting, scared to death and crying my eyes out. I'd felt like I'd been punched and kicked a few times in my life, but now I felt like an anvil had fallen on me.

I wish I could say that I was a better person than "Jenny" here—that the first thing through my mind was how sorry I was for poor Fred.

However, as I went running out of the armory, I was mostly thinking that *I* was going to die for sure now if I didn't become undead first. If Fred was dead, he certainly wouldn't be kissing me at the dance.

Naturally, when I got out the door, I found Gregory Grue standing in the parking lot and grinning. Grinning!

"Hoo hoo!" he said. "Blushing little green apple of my winking, blinking eye!"

"What the hell are you smiling about?" I asked.

"I'm not," he said, even though he was. "Shame about that poor kid, isn't it? Cut down in his prime!"

"You can't possibly expect me to get him to kiss me at the dance now," I said. "You've got to cancel the deal. It's only fair."

He shrugged his shoulders. "The moon wanes, and fate takes its cut, kiddo," he said. "This is just the way the pee dribbles in fairyland. The dance will end tomorrow night without you getting your kiss from Fred, and you'll drop dead. Nothing I can do, unless you decide to go with option B and get converted. I don't see what choice you have."

I'm pretty sure I was crying at this point. I don't know for sure—everything seems hazy when I try to remember this part of the story. My brain was running in a million directions at once and trying to get used to the fact that becoming a teenage vampire was necessary if I wanted to see another Thanksgiving.

Dying seemed like a better option, really. But if I was dead, Mutual might lose his resolve and agree to convert. I couldn't let that happen, even if I *would* be too dead to feel guilty.

Meanwhile, Gregory looked like he was having the time of his life. He grinned from ear to ear and breathed in deeply, like he hadn't smelled fresh air in years.

"So, I granted your wish, didn't I?" he said. "Cathy's going to spend her homecoming in a coma before waking up to a miserable eternity as a teenage member of the walking undead. She's lost her part in the show. She was in the running for valedictorian before, and that's totally out the window now. And you can bet that getting converted in the bathroom was not exactly the romantic adventure she always dreamed of. I did everything but throw her under a truck! How do you feel?"

"Awful," I said. "I have to live through an eternity of misery, too, if I convert!"

"Oh, it won't be so bad," he said. "I bet Mutual will decide to become a vampire, too, so he can be with you. At least you'll be miserable together! And you can get the Wells Fargo Wagon to school all by yourself."

"I can't believe this," I said. "I never wanted to be a vampire. Not even when every other girl did. And I can't believe Cathy got converted in the girls' bathroom. Disgusting."

"You won't have to do that," said Gregory. "Just step into your car tomorrow at any time. I'll have you drive out to a place where it can be done like a medical procedure. We'll put you to sleep first, so you won't even have to see the guy who does it."

I didn't say anything for a second.

"Is your friend part of Wilhelm's clan?" I asked.

"If he was, I wouldn't tell you, would I?" he replied. "If he was, the honor guard would be all over him, and you couldn't convert. You'd just have to die. Which I'd be okay with, but I'd rather have the money."

He was right. What was I going to do? Tell Murray, get the vampire friend taken out, and lose any chance I had of making it through the weekend myself?

It was over.

I had lost.

I was going to have to become a vampire the next day. There was no other option, besides just dying, which I wasn't brave enough to do. Then I'd have to hope Mutual got through the diciotto without finding out that I'd converted, which they'd surely use to convince him.

I sat down on the ground and just cried while Gregory Grue did his little dance.

After dancing, he crouched down, pulled a marker from his overcoat, and wrote something on my forehead.

His signature swear word, I assumed.

I was too weak and dazed to try to stop him, but after he finished, he went back to dancing around in the parking lot, and I crawled into my car and drove away. I paused only a minute to check the mirror to confirm the word he'd written was what I thought it was.

Even the dumbest of you probably realize that it's terribly humiliating to feel like you're totally broken and beaten *and* see a word like that on your forehead. I tried to wipe my tears with my hand, then use the tears to scrub it off, but it didn't do much good.

Finally, as I pulled out of the parking lot, I snapped.

I zipped down the road at way above the speed limit, screaming obscenities at the top of my lungs.

When I turned up the volume on the mix tape, it was playing a sort of calm song about trying to be free like a voice in a choir. I didn't want to calm down. I didn't want to be comforted.

I wanted to scream.

I fast-forwarded to the next song, which was faster, with a mean bass line and wicked keyboard part. It was another Leonard Cohen song, but it must have been from years later—his voice was a lot rougher, like he'd been through a few thousand packs of cigarettes since recording the calm song.

He was singing from the point of view of some criminal mastermind who planned to take over the world, starting with Manhattan and Berlin. It rocked pretty hard. When it ended I rewound and played it again.

I totally got this song, which I later found out was called "First We Take Manhattan."

The guy in the song had been sentenced to jail or something and now he was ready to get his revenge. By taking over the world.

He was going to break civilization just like I broke porcelain crap from the dollar store.

Man, that sounded good.

I needed to break something, too. And fast—if I became a super-strong vampire who could shatter a piece of junk just by touching it, swinging a crowbar probably wouldn't give me the same satisfaction. This was my last chance to get that aggression out of my system—I didn't want to take it into the afterlife with me.

But I also didn't want to just break more cheap junk. That wasn't going to be enough. I needed to break something *big*.

My first thought was to break the whole school, like getting Jason to use his pyro skills to build me a bomb and blowing the whole thing up. Not with anyone in it or anything—I didn't want to hurt anyone. But I wanted to wreck something huge.

Then I thought about maybe just breaking the damned dance.

And then my old debate-team instinct started to kick in,

working hand in hand with the parts of me that loved to fantasize about people dying violent deaths and stuff.

There was a loophole I hadn't noticed before.

The deal was that I had to get Fred to kiss me before the dance ended. I would die at the *end* of the dance.

So if the dance never ended, I wouldn't die.

And it couldn't end *if it didn't* start.

If there was no dance, I'd still be alive when Gregory Grue's allowance of magic wore out.

I felt like a string of Christmas lights was lighting up inside me, one at a time.

I could beat this.

Gregory Grue and his stupid spell were going to get *lawyered*!

And I was going to live. As a normal human.

I wasn't going to be able to do it alone, probably. It was going to be a lot of work to get the dance canceled, since they were still holding it despite everything that had already happened. I'd need help from people who wouldn't mind if the whole town wanted to kick their butts on Monday.

Luckily, I had a few friends who had been through that before.

And one who had experience with sabotage.

I rewound the tape to play "First We Take Manhattan" yet again, then turned my car toward Jason's house. As I did, I looked at the dirty word on my forehead and began to smile.

I had a plan.

"Okay," said Amber determinedly, "if you hit the gas hard, we should be able to bust right through the wall and save Fred!"

"Hold on tight!" Jenny yelled.

She stepped on the gas and rolled toward the brick wall. . . . Just as she did, her Prius stalled. It came to a stop an inch from the bricks. . . .

twenty-two

"Jenny" got lucky there. I am fairly sure that a Prius is not the kind of car that can break through a brick wall. She probably would have died in a brutal wreck.

As for the Jenmobile, it didn't stall once on the way to Jason's. As long as I played the tape, it ran like a dream. I later found out it was probably a residual-energy thing—I still don't understand it, but it's something like the way ghosts come to exist (another thing that used to be considered paranormal when I was a kid, but was pretty well explained since the post-humans went public).

The Jenmobile and I cruised clear to Jason's house, and I knocked on the door like I was trying to break it down. I saw his face peeking out the window before he let me in.

"Hey," he said. "What's going on? And what's with your forehead?"

"Never mind the forehead, I need your help, fast," I said.

"What's up?"

"Did you hear about the vampire-on-vampire murder today?"

"Sure," said Jason. "Some vampire attacked another one. It happens."

"It was Fred," I said.

"What?" asked Jason. "Fred is *dead?*"

I nodded, and choked back a few tears. While Jason sat down on the couch, looking like he'd just been punched in the face, I took a second to hope that Fred was better off wherever he was now. He practically had to be, really. He hadn't wanted to live forever.

But there was no time for mourning. Not yet.

Mutual came wandering up from the basement, still looking freaked out.

"Did you just say Fred got killed?" he asked.

I nodded and sniffled a bit.

"Do they know who did it?"

"Not yet," I said. "I assume it was someone from Will's clan. A couple of guys are heading up to Canada to check on them."

"Wait," said Jason. "If Fred is dead, then . . ."

"Then he sure as hell isn't going to be taking me to homecoming," I said. "But I have a plan. I can sit back and die, agree to become a vampire, or do something totally extraordinary."

"What?"

"The deal with Gregory was that I had to get Fred to kiss me before the dance *ended*. If the dance never starts, it can't end, and I'm home free."

"So you want to get it canceled?" asked Jason. "They already said they're not letting the attack or the whole thing with Cathy get in the way, or we'd just be letting them win. I don't know what'll get it canceled if a student getting killed doesn't. Unless you want to bomb the school or something."

I smiled. "We don't have a bomb, but we've got a unicorn and a lot of . . . the word on my forehead. And a Wells Fargo Wagon. How long do you think it would take to get the smell of unicorn poop out of the gym?"

A smile spread across Jason's face.

"I get it," he said. "You think we should roll a wagon full of unicorn crap to school and spread it around the gym so they won't want to have the dance there?"

"Well, I don't want it in my car!" I said. "I'd never get the smell out and I can't afford a new one. But we could load up the wagon with it and use the unicorn to drive it there. I need to get it to the school somehow, anyway."

"Oh man, that's brilliant," said Jason. "Fred would have *loved* it."

"We'll do it for him," I said. "The Fred-the-Vampire Memorial Vandalism Initiative. Let's go get Amber!"

"I'm coming with you," said Mutual.

"The hell you are," I said. "You stay right here where it's safe. There are probably some bad people out there besides your parents right now."

"Yeah, man," said Jason. "I don't think there's any law about trespassing in moving Wells Fargo Wagons. They might even already have permission for the diciotto. They could do it right in the wagon."

Mutual kicked the floor, then collapsed onto the couch.

"I'm sorry," I called out as Jason and I ran for my car.

I played that song about the criminal as loudly as I could as we cruised up through Preston and picked up Amber. Jason shouted what I'd told him into her ear while I drove us to my house.

"Let's do it!" she said. "In memory of Fred!"

"For Fred!" I agreed.

I parked in the street, and we got out and I walked them up to the Wells Fargo Wagon.

"Amber," I said, "you grew up on a horse ranch. Can you get a unicorn hitched up to a wagon?"

"Yes with a capital Hell," said Amber.

"Good," I said. "You guys work on hitching her up, and I'll be right back."

I ran inside and found three old T-shirts, then sprayed them all with perfume from my mother's bathroom cabinet.

After tying the first shirt around my nose and mouth, I ran outside. On the way, I caught a glimpse of myself in the mirror: purple sweatshirt, purple hair, purple bandana.

I looked like a Batman villain.

Outside, Amber had managed to get Princess out and get the leash or harness or whatever set up. I tossed them the other shirts to tie around their faces, and we grabbed the shovels from the shed, transporting all the mess out to the wagon one shovelful at a time.

It was amazing how much Princess had generated. Another few days and she could have drowned.

Now, *there* we have an awful way to die.

The perfume covered the stench about halfway, which was barely enough to keep me from barfing, but it was enough, since I was determined to get the job done. It was life and death for me—I was really touched that Jason and Amber were willing to go through all this for my sake, too.

"Pretty nasty, huh?" Amber shouted through her bandana.

"I never promised you a rose garden," said Jason.

It took about nine trips each to get all the mess transferred from the shed to the wagon. Once it was all there, piled high and deep, we tossed the tools under the seat and Amber shook the reins, but Princess didn't budge.

"Damn," she said. "How do you start these things?"

Just then, we heard the sound of screeching tires, and Jason's car came barreling up the road. It came to a roaring stop right in front of my house, and Mutual stepped out.

"What are you doing?" I asked. "You can drive?"

"No different from a tractor," he said. "Well, not too different. Sorry I borrowed it without asking, Jason."

"No problem," said Jason. "But you should have stayed indoors."

"Hurry up and get inside my house," I said. "You're not safe out here!"

"No," he said. "I'm not missing this."

"But it's dangerous!"

He left the car in the road and came walking up the driveway, his long hair blowing in the autumn breeze. Damn, he looked hot.

"I didn't come twenty-five hundred miles in a bus to live in a basement for five to ten years," he said. "If they're coming, let them come. What good am I anyway if I can't stand up to a couple of stupid Victorians?"

"Are you sure?" I asked. "There's a killer on the loose, you know."

"I know. But I'm not missing this. I owe it to you, to Fred, and to myself to be a part of it. I'll never forgive myself if I chicken out. If I'm gonna get caught or killed, it's gonna be while I'm with you guys, not sitting in a basement."

I looked at him for a second, and the look on his face told me that this wasn't negotiable.

"You want me to go get a bandana for you?"

"I'm a farm kid," he said. "I can take it. We had some hybrids. They all smell like this."

This was the Mutual I had been waiting for.

The strong one who came swooping in to save me.

Not that I wasn't prepared to save myself or anything, but he was finally looking like the gutsy kid I'd fallen for. The dork with a heart of fire and gold.

Only, now he was new and improved.

Mutual Scrivener: now with 300 percent more muscles. He was back, and he meant business.

He hopped up to the wagon, took the reins from Amber, and shouted something. Princess began to trot, and the wagon rolled out of the driveway and into the street at a slow but steady pace.

Soon we were riding through the streets of Preston toward Cornersville Trace, in a unicorn-led cart full of the smelliest stuff in the world.

Well, I thought, *I wanted to have an unusual life!*

I sang out "The Wells Fargo Wagon" song all the way up Jacqueline Terrace, making up new lines as we went along. There are a lot of lines in the song where people talk about what they've gotten from the wagon, like grapefruits from Tampa and bathtubs from Montgomery Ward. I changed those to reflect what they'd be getting this time, which was . . . well, you know. Not a double boiler or a new rocking chair.

I'd never been more disgusted. But I'd also never felt more alive.

As we topped the hill, I could see the tops of the tallest couple of buildings in downtown Des Moines, ten miles away, like silent sentinels.

When I finished the song, I looked over at Mutual.

"You really sure you want to do this?" I asked. "We'll probably attract attention. We can get you back to Jason's house if we hurry."

Mutual shook his head, braced himself, stood up as well as he could on the front of the wagon, and launched into the St. Crispin's Day speech from *Henry V.*

> *"He which hath no stomach to this fight,*
> *Let him depart; his passport shall be made*
> *And crowns for convoy put into his purse:*
> *We would not die in that man's company*
> *That fears his fellowship to die with us."*

My God, my heart was melting.

He wasn't just muttering the lines, he was shouting as loudly as he could.

He paused for a second and nodded his head up and down, like he was trying to remember the rest of the speech, then kept on shouting.

"This day is call'd the feast of Crispian:
He that outlives this day, and comes safe home,
Will stand a tip-toe when this day is named,
He . . . will . . . strip his sleeve and show his scars,
And say 'These wounds I had on Crispin's day.'"

"We few, we band of brothers!" I shouted. "They will tell our story! And our names will be as familiar in their mouths as household words!"

That was the only part of the speech I could remember, and it wasn't even quite right.

But Mutual remembered more. He kept on shouting.

"We few, we happy few, we band of brothers; . . .
Gentlemen in England now a-bed
Shall think themselves accursed they were not here,
And hold their manhoods cheap while any speaks
That fought with us upon Saint Crispin's Day."

I watched him standing there, hollering Shakespeare lines without seeming even a little embarrassed or afraid of seeming like a brainiac or whatever. Standing defiant.

I couldn't remember any more of the speech, so I just shouted "*Yaaa!*" into the night.

And then Mutual shouted, "*Yaaa!*"

And then Amber and Jason joined in, shouting whatever they could think to shout along with us as we rolled into the night.

"Onward to glory!" Jason shouted.

"Remember the *Maine* and to hell with Spain!" shouted Amber.

"First we take Manhattan, then we take Berlin!" I yelled.

"Four score and seven years ago!" Jason shouted.

"I obfuscate by night!" Mutual shouted.

And then it got weirder as we shouted TV catchphrases, more Shakespeare, a couple of commercial slogans—whatever we could think of.

I don't think Henry V's army was exactly out to get a dance canceled using a wagon full of unicorn crap, or afraid they might have to face the wrath of angry vampires or fairy curses.

And I'm sure that when Henry told his army that their story would make them famous, he didn't mean they would make a book like *Born to Be Extraordinary* that left out all the messy parts.

But the idea was the same.

We few, we happy few.

We band of brothers.

Mutual and I leaned over and kissed, again and again, as we rolled along.

I knew I might not survive the weekend if this caper didn't work out. Or even if it did. Maybe lawyering my way out of this wouldn't break the spell.

And maybe Mutual wasn't going to be able to get through the diciotto, and I'd wish I'd become a vampire myself when I had the chance.

Anything was possible.

But at least if I lost, I'd lose fighting.

And if I died, I'd die an extraordinary death.

Maybe some people are born to be extraordinary, and maybe you can become extraordinary on your own, but if you ask me, it's probably impossible. Unless you're being raised by a family of rich eccentrics (like the women in those movies usually are), you'll probably need a few friends to help.

Friends who can keep you smiling and brave when you're just days away from dying due to a fairy curse if you don't complete some mysterious task.

Friends who are willing to risk their lives to help save yours.

Friends who are willing to take off their perfumed bandanas and shout into the night even when you're riding in the stinkiest of all possible wagons.

And if you can make out with one of them after you're done screaming into the bitter Iowa night, well, all the better.

As Fred leaned in and gave Jenny the kiss she'd longed for, she felt herself change. She was a princess. A fairy princess. She'd never felt so wonderful, so pure, so beautiful. She finally felt extraordinary.

When she opened her eyes, sparks were flying across the dance floor.

twenty-three

So, well, it wasn't sparks flying across the dance floor on the night I first felt truly extraordinary. It was poop. Lots and lots of unicorn poop.

After a few minutes, it was all over the gym floor.

There was some hidden in the vents.

More was dripping from the light fixtures, and more still was splattered against the backboards of the basketball hoops.

I used my crowbar like a baseball bat, balancing one big glob on the end of it, then swinging it to send the glob flying up against a trophy case. Then I used it like a golf club to spread the mess around on the floor and to smash some of the breakable stuff around the gym.

I'd been trying to get away from all that destruction business, but I figured it was okay when it was a matter of life and death.

I was probably looking at a stiff fine, and possibly a short jail sentence, along with maybe screwing up my scholarships and stuff. The crowbar sure as hell violated the zero-tolerance rule, and we were vandalizing school property, which was obviously frowned on. I doubted that anyone would believe I'd done it to get out of a deal with a fairy godmother.

But it's funny how little stuff like that matters when there's a chance that you're about to die. I just kept flinging crap all over the place.

And what *Music Man* song was running through my head the whole time? Why, "Shipoopi," of course!

Soon, the gym was the stinkiest, nastiest place imaginable. There was no way they could ever hold a dance there without airing it out, which could take weeks. They'd have to cancel the dance—or at least postpone it until after Gregory's magic had worn off. I'd be amazed if we didn't miss a few days of school, too.

I can't imagine I'll ever live through anything more disgusting. I sure hope not.

But, yeah, in a weird way, I *did* feel beautiful.

When we had flung the last of the mess, I turned Princess loose in the football field and just left her there to stink it up while the four of us made a run for it, leaving the wagon behind.

I raised my crowbar above my head and yelled in triumph as we fled.

We jogged clear down the road to the Penguin Foot Creamery, the ice cream shop on Cedar Avenue, and stepped inside.

"Four grape sodas, please," I said to the clerk.

He took a step back. I had forgotten that we stank.

"We'll sit *way* over there, by the door," I told him.

"I'd kind of rather you sat outside," he said.

"It's not safe out there," said Jason. "If a couple of vampires who look like they have rods up their butts show up, reserve the right to refuse them service, okay? We're on the run."

"Will you at least leave the crowbar outside?" he asked.

"Done," I said.

I stashed it outside the front door, then took a seat with the three of them at the booth farthest away from the counter, where we gave each other high fives and raised a toast to Fred.

"Fred," I shouted, "this was all for you!"

"To Fred!" Jason called out.

Mutual and Amber raised their glasses, too.

"No shouting, please!" said the clerk.

One of the things I sort of regret about telling this story now is that we only told people that Mutual was Fred *partly* to keep Mutual from being harassed. We also let a whole generation think that Fred the vampire was a total hunk as a sort of tribute to him. We think he'd be amused. I kind of hate to let that go.

After we each had a long sip in his honor, I pulled out my phone and gave Murray a call.

"Any word from the guys in Canada?" I asked.

"They're there now," he said. "And all the guys from Will's clan are accounted for and under guard."

"Do they think it was one of them who killed Fred?"

"That's still our working theory," said Murray, "but we don't know how, because none of them has a blood scent that matched the one at the scene."

"So the killer's still in town? And whoever converted Cathy?"

"Maybe," he said, "but Will's clan was the only group that we would have suspected would also go after the dance. If it was anyone else, it was an inside job. Maybe someone he owed money to, we don't know. The important thing, though, is you're safe, and we're still on call. So don't worry, okay?"

"Thanks," I said.

I hung up the phone as Mutual finished his grape soda and crushed the cup against his forehead. He still seemed a bit bummed when we mentioned Fred, but other than that, I'd never seen him so animated or happy.

"Man," he said. "I've been waiting for years for a chance to do something like that again!"

"You're really seeming alive tonight," said Amber. "No offense, but you sort of seemed beat up until now."

"Hey," Mutual said. "I was on a series of buses and boats for a week to get here. You try looking alive after that!"

"Nothing like vandalism to stir your spirits," said Jason.

I suddenly remembered that Mutual had mentioned a twenty-five-hundred-mile bus trip earlier, at Jason's house. I'd been so busy with the plan that I hadn't noticed it at the time.

"So, wait, you took the bus out here?" I asked. "I assumed you flew!"

He shook his head. "I had to drive a tractor to Anchorage just to get started. Then the ticket got me on a bus to a seaport, a boat to Seattle, then another bus all the way to Des Moines, and a cab out to Preston."

"Wow," I said. "How long did that take?"

"Six days," he said casually. "We had to stop at every little town with a bus stop along the way!"

That was odd. If he'd been on the road for that long before arriving on Monday, that meant he had already been on his way when I'd first met Gregory. Mutual had to have gotten the ticket before I'd made any wishes.

So the postcard on the wagon was just a crazy, unbelievable coincidence? Maybe Gregory had found it in the wagon earlier, when it was still wherever it was before he delivered it, and *assumed* I'd want Mutual to come back, and sent the ticket before I'd even made the wish?

That seemed like a stretch.

"Who do you think got you the ticket?" I asked.

"I sort of assumed it was one of you guys, actually," he said. "When you said it wasn't, I guessed it must have been . . . I don't know. Someone who still wanted to kick my butt over losing the spelling bee in person or something. But I would have taken a ticket from the devil himself to get here."

"It could have even been Mrs. Smollet," said Jason. "She might have wanted you here so she could get Jennifer involved in the diciotto."

"I thought about that, too," said Mutual. "She's probably my main suspect so far."

Just then, my phone buzzed. The number came up as "unknown," but I knew it would be Gregory before I even answered.

"What the hell is going on?" he roared. "I just heard something about a unicorn at the school!"

"What's going on is that *you* just got lawyered!" I said. "The dance is never going to end now, because it isn't going to start!"

"No one lawyers me!" he growled. "Especially not some stupid, ordinary little girl who isn't even a freaking lawyer. I'm back behind the Creamery. Meet me. Now. You didn't solve the puzzle, you just made things worse! *Worse!* You're going to regret this, girly girl."

I felt like someone had punched me in the gut. Then kicked me in the face and pulled me around by my hair.

I told Jason, Amber, and Mutual that I would be right back, and ran around outside and behind the building. Gregory was waiting for me, leaning against the wall and holding up an unlit cigar.

"Hoo hoo," he said. He was being much more curt than usual.

I'd never seen him look so . . . evil. His face was glowing red in the light from the gas station sign next door.

But I tried my best to screw my courage to the sticking place.

"Lawyered," I said.

"The law is an ass," he replied. "I'd say that more likely, the minute they announce homecoming is canceled, you'll just drop dead. These spells are harder to predict than a horse race, but the deck tends to be stacked against humans."

"The deal was that I had to get kissed before the dance ended," I said. "And now that it won't start—"

"Not how it works!" he growled. "People from the school board are going to get to the scene of your little crime spree any second. As soon as they take a whiff, they'll cancel the dance. And once they do, you'll die. And so will Mutual."

"Mutual?"

"He's mixed up in this, too. And if you *ever* kiss him again without both of you being undead, you'll both die. Those are two new rules I'm adding as a punishment for this little stunt!"

"You're changing the rules!" I said. "First you say you can't predict it, then you change the rules!"

"It can't be helped," he said. He held up his unlit cigar and twirled it in his fingers like a baton. "You've got no choice left. I can still get you both converted if we hurry, but once they cancel that dance, it's too late. You'll just be faces in the smoke."

"You're bluffing," I said. "He didn't even sign a letter of intent."

"His parents signed one for him years ago, when he was still a minor. And I have consent forms ready for both of you. Go explain all this to him, and I can get you both handled without him having to deal with a diciotto. It's better this way. Trust me."

For a split second, I wondered how the hell he knew Mutual's parents had signed a letter for him. But he didn't give me any more time to think about it—he chewed on the unlit cigar and paced back and forth while his grin got wider and wider.

"If I blow a puff of this in your face, you'll be asleep in a few minutes," he said. "Took about five for Cathy to be out."

"Did you have a spell going with her, too?"

He laughed. "It was part of how I made your little wish

come true," he said. "I told her *she'd* die, too if you didn't kiss her boyfriend at the dance. Ha! The little brat had to break up with him herself!"

He started laughing so hard he was literally clutching his sides.

His story made sense, as far as I could tell. It explained why Cathy had broken up with Fred *right* after her meeting with Gregory about getting her part back. And why she was so determined to set me up with him.

"And that scheme she came up with!" he said. "Telling him you were dying of some dread disease?"

"She did *what?*"

"He was taking you to the dance because he thought you were oozing gunk out of every pore, growing tumors on every limb, and that you'd be dead before Christmas. A completely idiotic scheme! You probably thought she was telling him you'd do all sorts of naughty things, huh? Like he'd want to do them with *you!*"

I felt my stomach knotting up and my cheeks burning.

"And the best part," said Gregory between his gales of laughter, "is that her stupid plan actually worked better than anything your peanut brain came up with! Or it would have, if Fred wasn't in several pieces right now."

"So that's why she converted," I said. "You told her Fred died, and she thought she'd die if she didn't convert, since I couldn't kiss him at the dance. Did you make a few bucks off it from your vampire friend?"

The little booger grinned at me. "What's that line from *Music Man?* The thing about the piper?"

"From the first song?" I asked.

"Yeah."

"'When the man dances, certainly, boys, what else? The piper pays him.'"

"That's me!" said Gregory, as he went into dancing one of his little jigs. "When I dance, certainly, boys, what else? The piper pays me! Now go get your boyfriend and tell him it's time to get converted. Hoo hoo!"

I started to wander back to the front of the store.

This didn't make any sense. He was changing the rules on me! He had said before that he couldn't control things that well, and now he was acting like he could.

And he was lying outright about getting Mutual a ticket *after* I wished for him.

And then I thought of the last thing he said.

The thing about the piper.

It was a line about Harold Hill. A con artist.

I felt like there were wheels in my head that were starting to turn. I could hear the clink of the gears and everything.

Gregory had to have known Mutual was on his way to town. There was no way his showing up—as the result of a mysterious ticket—could be a coincidence. And if Gregory had sent him the ticket before he spoke to me, it wouldn't have been magical.

But Gregory could have dropped off the ticket himself. And picked up a postcard to leave in the wagon while he was at it.

And how did he know about Mutual's parents signing him a letter of intent? Had Smollet told him?

Pieces began to fit together as I walked back into the ice cream shop.

Click. Click. Click.

"Where did you go?" asked Amber, when I made it back to the booth. "Did you pee behind the bushes or something?"

"I hate these places that don't have a bathroom," said Jason.

I shook my head.

"Are you okay?" Amber asked.

I just sat there for a second, thinking.

"Hello?" said Amber. "Earth to Jennifer!"

I turned to Mutual.

"You don't have any money," I said.

"No. I ran out in Nebraska."

"But you took a cab to Jason's house, all the way from downtown to Preston. How could you afford the fare?"

"I didn't have to pay," he said. "Some cabdriver offered me a free ride from the Greyhound station."

"Was it a short guy?"

"Yeah. He had to sit on a stack of phone books just to see over the dashboard. I think I saw him in that bar we went into with Fred, but I was too nervous to say hi to him, and he was gone when Fred and I came back inside."

Click, click, click.

"Was it the same guy who brought you the FedEx package with the ticket?"

"I don't think so," said Mutual. "That guy was all bundled up—but he was pretty short, come to think of it."

"And did you give him a postcard hoping he'd mail it?"

"Of course. I gave everyone I possibly could a postcard for you. I used to keep one in my pocket all the time, just in case."

Click, click, click.

Gregory was definitely behind everything that had happened that week.

And the fact that the terms of the spell seemed to change, along with the rules about whether they *could* be changed, was fishy as hell.

I let the wheels in my head turn until I had put the pieces together. Once I got the first few, the rest fell into place almost on their own. I felt like the biggest idiot in the world for not figuring it out sooner.

But I was no "stupid, ordinary little girl."

And Gregory Grue was no fairy godmother.

He was a barefaced, double-shuffle, two-bit, thimble-rigging, sick bastard con artist who tricked girls into thinking they would die if they didn't consent to become vampires!

In fact, he must have been a vampire himself. If he was the kind who could play tricks on people's brains, it would explain almost everything he had done that seemed magical. All the vanishing glitter, faces in smoke—everything could have just been an illusion. He probably even sent the dreams about Fred into my head.

And considering what he'd had Fred do in those dreams, this guy was *way* out of line.

There was no vampire buddy. Just him. He was the one doing the converting. As soon as the idea occurred to me, I was sure I was right. I felt a bead of sweat run down the side of my face and a sharp pain in my sinuses.

"You okay?" asked Mutual.

"Let me think a few more seconds."

Click, click, click.

Maybe he had even come after me with the full blessing of Mutual's parents, so that when I converted, they'd have that as leverage on him. That would explain how he had known they'd signed a letter of intent for him when he was a minor. And why he'd sent Mutual to Iowa to start with.

I still didn't know where he'd gotten the unicorn, but I was certain there was no spell that would kill me at the end of the dance. Or if I kissed Mutual again.

Vampires couldn't do "magic." Just cheap tricks.

I looked over at Mutual, Jason, and Amber.

"Uh, guys?" I said. "I think we may have just trashed the school for nothing."

"Are you kidding?" said Jason. "This is going to freak people out!"

"It's the most amazing night of my life," said Amber. "Fred would be proud of you!"

"But we didn't need to do it," I said. "I wouldn't have died. There's no fairy curse or anything going on here. It's all just a trick to make me convert so Mutual will." I frowned. "And I think I know who killed Fred. Just to make sure I wouldn't be able to kiss him."

"What?" said Amber. "Who?"

"Gregory Grue is no fairy godmother," I said. "Or any other kind of fairy. He's a fake! And he doesn't know the territory!"

"What?" said Jason.

"He killed Fred and converted Cathy, and he paid for Mutual's ticket and then gave him a free cab ride."

"It was that guy?" asked Mutual. "*That* was the guy who said he was a fairy godmother? The cabdriver?"

"Yeah," I said. "I think so. He wants to trick me into

converting so *you* will. He might even be working for your parents."

"Well, I knew that guy was a vampire," said Mutual. "There was an empty can of VS Thirty-Two in his cup holder in the cab!"

"See?" I shouted. "He just told me we'd both die if I ever kissed you again, but I think he was just trying to scare us both into converting. Do you feel like taking a chance?"

He nodded.

"It's life or death," I said. "I'm sure I'm right, but if I'm wrong, we'll both drop dead."

"I don't care," he said. "It's worth it."

And I leaned over, grabbed the back of his head, closed my eyes, and pulled him toward me, giving him the biggest, sloppiest, most passionate kiss I possibly could.

As Fred's lips pressed against hers, Jenny—Princess Jenny—felt herself changing. She felt the world changing. She felt her soul touching his.

twenty-four

Actually, change the names around and that would be just about right. That's exactly what that kiss felt like.

After I ran out of breath, I pulled back and looked down at my hands, as one does when one is checking to see if one is still alive.

They were still there.

"Still breathing?" I asked Mutual.

He nodded. "Yeah. Yeah with a capital Hell."

I laughed—it was still weird to hear Mutual use even the most minor swear words.

"So where's this Grue guy now?" asked Jason. "I'll kick his ass clear back to Alaska!"

"No offense, but he'd hand yours back to you," I said. "He may be short, but he's still a vampire. Let me get the honor guard. This fairy godmofo's going *down*."

"How long until they can get here?" asked Mutual.

"I'll text Murray and they'll be here as soon as he gets the message," I said. "If Gregory comes in, just stall him. Don't tell him we're on to him or there's no telling what he might do."

I took out my phone and began to type a text message:

```
GREGORY GRUE IS NOT A FAIRY, HE'S
A VAMPIRE CON MAN. KILLED FRED.
OUT TO CONVERT ME. BEHIND PENGUIN
FOOT CREAMERY ON CEDAR AVE. I AM
INSIDE. SEND HEL
```

I wasn't quite done when I heard a cough and looked up to see Gregory standing at our table.

"Hoo hoo," he said. "What's taking you so long?"

"Just clearing up our affairs," I said.

"No need," he said. And he grabbed my phone out of my hand and slipped it into the inside pocket of his overcoat. "Better let me hang on to that for you," he said. "It can mess with a conversion. Just like taking them on airplanes."

"That's odd," I said. "I've never heard that before."

"Now," he said, "let's get down to business before it's too late. I called that Smollet woman, so school officials are heading for the gym right now."

He reached into his coat and pulled out two sheets of paper—letters of consent—from the same pocket where he was keeping my phone. I had to get that phone back, and fast.

"Here we are," he said. "Now, if you two could just hurry on up, I'll see about getting you to sleep for the big operation."

And he reached into another pocket and pulled out his cigar. The one that would put me to sleep.

"I don't think you need to do that," I said. "I'd actually rather stay conscious."

"Me too," said Mutual. "I don't like to lose control of myself."

"Yeah," said Jason. "This is a drug-free zone around here, pal!"

"Shut up," said Gregory. "This doesn't concern you!"

Meanwhile, I was trying to think of what the heck Murray's phone number was so I could say it out loud or write it down on the form and hope Amber would notice and call it.

Gregory pulled out a match, lit it, and brought it to the cigar. It was barely an inch away when the clerk shouted out, "No smoking!"

"Don't mind us," Jason told him. "We're all just leaving. Right?"

"Thank God," said the guy.

"You shouldn't talk about your customers like that," said Jason. "That's pretty lousy customer service."

"You got a mouth on you, kid," Gregory said to Jason. Then he turned to the clerk. "We'll get outside as soon as these two sign the papers."

"No," said the clerk. "Right now. They can sign them on the picnic tables out there. I want you out of my store."

Gregory rolled his eyes.

"Let's go, kids," he said. "I'd hate to have this kid get the assistant manager. I hate everything about assistant managers except their sweet, crunchity taste."

We all stood up and wandered outside. All the while, I

thought of ways to get my phone out of Gregory's pocket. I let him out the door first, then turned back to the clerk.

"Call the police, please," I said.

"I don't think I'll need to go that far," he said.

Damn.

When I got out, Gregory lit his cigar.

"Hold on," I said. "I think we should sign the forms first. That cigar might put us to sleep before we can sign."

"Well, hurry it up," he said.

He laid the forms on the little picnic table and set out a couple of pens.

I figured that if I signed, he'd have to open his coat back up to put it back inside. Granting this guy consent to convert me was the absolute last thing in the world I wanted to do, but it might have been my only chance to get him caught.

"Come on," he said. "No time like the present. Not to rush you, but I have a train to catch this evening."

"Getting out of town?" I asked. "Without even finishing the show?"

"Hate to break it to you, kiddo," he said. "You won't be seeing me again."

"You're just like Harold Hill, all right."

"Hey, Harold Hill improved the lives of those dumb Iowans," he said. "Just like I'm improving yours!"

I took a deep breath. It was easy to imagine that in earlier days, Gregory might have been a crooked traveling salesman. I'll bet lots of vampires were—it was a perfect job for them. You never had to stay anywhere long enough for people to realize you weren't aging.

"So, how's this going to work?" I asked as I pretended to read over the form. "I sign, you put me to sleep, then you cart me away?"

"That's right," he said.

"What about me?" said Mutual. "Who's going to do the operation on me?"

"I'll have my buddy get in touch with your parents," said Gregory. "They've got someone in mind, right?"

Mutual cringed.

"That's what I thought," said Gregory. "They'll be here in seconds, I'm sure. You can just sleep on this table or something. It'll be good for your back!"

"Well," I said, "I guess I'd better hurry, then."

And I walked up to the picnic table and signed my name on the form. Gregory grinned, took a drag on his cigar, and blew a puff in my face.

I tried not to inhale, but my eyelids felt heavy immediately.

"There you go," he said. "Have a seat at the table and just relax. You'll be out like a light in a few minutes."

And he set my form on the table.

"Okay," he said. "One down, one to go."

He turned toward Mutual and I leaned in to Jason. "Get ready to act," I said. "If we can distract him for even a second, grab that phone!"

Gregory turned back to me. I'd forgotten how well he could hear.

"Still out to get your phone back?" he asked.

"I should really call my mom," I said, "just to keep her from worrying about me."

"I'll take care of it," he said. "I'm a teacher, after all."

My eyelids got heavier and heavier.

Gregory turned away again, and I saw Jason mouthing the words "Distract him!" at Mutual.

I felt like I had maybe a minute before I'd be out cold.

But a plan suddenly came to me. I looked at Mutual and jerked my head toward the paper, hoping he understood what I meant.

"Okay," said Mutual. "I'll sign."

Bingo.

Gregory just watched as Mutual very, very slowly signed his name on the form. Though I was so tired I felt like I had sandbags attached to every limb, I took a few slow and careful steps to the side, to the space by the door where I'd left my crowbar, and grabbed it.

Gregory had forgotten that I was awfully handy with a crowbar.

As Mutual finished signing, Gregory blew cigar smoke into his face. I took a tiny step toward the mofo, creeping up slowly and carefully behind him to keep him from noticing.

"That won't do it," said Mutual. "I'll need another puff."

"It should be plenty," said Gregory.

"No," said Mutual. "One more."

Gregory blew in his face again. Mutual looked more tired to me than he had ever been, but he said, "Bigger than that!"

"You're one tough cookie," said Gregory. "But if you insist!"

And he took a big enough puff that Mutual's entire body was surrounded by smoke, along with most of Gregory's.

With the last of my strength, I jumped forward and swung my crowbar into Gregory's ankle.

Since he was a vampire and could have walked off a gunshot, it didn't do much damage.

But it distracted him.

"Hey!" he shouted. "What the hell are you doing?"

While he turned around, Jason and I both moved to grab the phone out of his pocket.

Neither of us made it. Gregory just stepped aside, and we both ended up crashing to the ground.

"Not smart," Gregory said. "Not smart at all."

"Uh, you guys?" said Amber. "Mutual's gone."

I looked over to the spot where the puff of smoke had been. The smoke was disturbed, like someone had run through it, but there was no sign of Mutual.

Gregory grinned down at me. "His parents probably watched this whole thing," he said. "And they came and got him as soon as he signed that form!"

Oh God. I had failed.

Mutual was probably on his way to Alaska.

"Give me my phone!" I gasped.

"What is the deal with this little toy?" he asked. And he reached into his pocket, took out the phone, and looked at the message I'd been sending.

"Give it!" I said as my vision began to get blurry. I was fighting to keep my eyes open, and there was no way I could wield a crowbar again.

Behind me, I heard the Penguin Foot clerk shouting, "No fighting! Get out of here before I call the cops."

Everyone ignored him.

"So, you solved the mystery, did you?" Gregory growled as he read the text. "Figured out old Gregory's secret."

"Did Mutual's parents send you?" I asked him.

"I guess I don't have to convert you now," he said. "Now that they got what they wanted. But since you signed the form, I might as well. . . ."

"Prove it!" shouted Amber. And she belched.

Gregory and I turned our heads and saw that she was holding up the two consent forms. The signatures had been ripped off, and I guess she had eaten them.

"Spit them out!" shouted Gregory. "Or I'll cut you open to get them! I'll bite you! I will!"

"I wouldn't," said a voice with a New York accent.

I looked behind Gregory and saw Murray, Mrs. Smollet, and several people from the honor guard.

Murray and a few others vanished, then reappeared holding Gregory down on the table.

"He killed Fred!" Jason shouted. "Check the scent!"

One of the vampires took a whiff of the air around Gregory, like a drug dog, then vanished.

While the three of them struggled with Gregory, I turned to Smollet, who was standing and watching the whole scene, looking terrified.

"Where's Mutual?" I asked her.

She took a few steps toward me. "When I heard about the unicorn, I followed my nose and found you all here," she said. "I brought Mutual to his parents, but when I came back to get the consent form, Gregory was threatening you, so I called in the guard."

"He's with his parents?" I asked, fighting to stay conscious. "Get him back here! There's no consent form anymore!"

"And if they hired this guy, they were *way* over the line," she said.

And she vanished.

The vampire who had been sniffing the air reappeared. "It was him!" he shouted. "His smell is all over Fred's apartment!"

"Let me go!" bellowed Gregory. "I am a Person of Peace!"

"Somebody get the council on the phone and get us permission to deal with this joker," Murray called. "I'm not having another vampire attack. Not in my town."

Gregory broke away from the three by slipping out of his coat, but got intercepted by a vampire on the other end of the lot when he tried to run. He disappeared off the table, then reappeared fighting with the other guy. The two of them moved so fast that they looked like they were just flickering in and out of existence.

Meanwhile, I got woozier and woozier.

I didn't even have the energy left to turn my head when I heard the clerk shouting, "I'm calling the cops!"

Violence in my head is one matter, but at that moment I realized for sure that I'm no fan of the real thing. Any worry that I really *wanted* the people I fantasized about killing to be brutally murdered vanished right then and there.

The last thing I heard before I passed out was the sound of Mutual's mother saying, "I know your tricks and manners," as the Penguin Foot guy shouted, "They're coming!"

And then everything went black, and all I heard was this roar that sounded like the ocean.

I felt like I'd been asleep for hours when I woke up a few minutes later. I was sitting upright on one of the picnic table benches, and my head was surrounded by smoke.

"There," said Murray, who was holding a cigar that smelled different from any I'd seen Gregory smoke. "That should wake her."

"I'm up," I said. "Where's Mutual?"

"He's fine," said Jason, who was beside me. "He's totally safe. But don't look at the parking lot."

I looked in the opposite direction and saw a few vampires holding Mutual's parents' hands behind their backs.

"What would you have us do?" asked his mother. "Watch our only child grow old and die?"

"Yes!" shouted Amber. "That's what people are supposed to do, you pumpkin-sucking goons!"

I turned toward Amber and saw that Mutual was propped up next to her, fast asleep.

"He'll be okay, right?" I asked.

"Oh, yeah," said Murray. "But I can't wake him right up from three large puffs of that stuff Gregory had in the cigar. He'll be asleep for a few hours, at least."

"Thank God," I said. "He took two extra puffs to keep Gregory busy while I snuck up on him with a crowbar."

Murray chuckled a bit. "Three puffs! That's a brave kid."

Smollet turned to me. "I'm sorry, Jennifer," she said. "I didn't know."

I remembered that she had apologized to Alley after she got attacked, too.

"You know what?" I said. "You could be a really good person if someone was just being attacked by a vampire every minute of the day."

I was probably being meaner than I should have been, considering she'd just saved my ass by calling the council.

Of course, Gregory had saved it, too, by calling to tell

her about the unicorn. I guess that was just supposed to scare me into thinking the clock was ticking, but it had totally backfired on him.

Smollet sighed, and I heard the voice of the Penguin Foot Creamery guy shouting, "I warned you!" I looked down Cedar Avenue and saw an ambulance and what must have been every police car in town coming up the road.

When they pulled into the parking lot, the sirens scared away a whole flock of blackbirds that flew off into the night.

Then I saw why Jason had told me not to look in the parking lot.

They had been pecking away at what was left of Gregory Grue.

His fedora was perched on a car antenna. I stared at it for a long, long time.

And so Princess Jenny went home to her house to run the kingdom from afar, while she waited to find girls who could join her on the royal court . . . girls who were born to be extraordinary, just like her. . . .

twenty-five

There's no happily-ever-after, really.

My story could have ended a few times—like, after I got the date with Fred. Or after we wrecked the gym. But it didn't. Life is too interesting for that. There was always something coming up next.

After a few days of mourning and recovery, it felt like we'd gotten to happily-ever-after for a while, since Gregory was defeated and the council had called off the diciotto. When the dust had settled and everything had calmed down, there really were a couple of good, happy months before the book came out.

Mutual's parents swore they had no idea just how bad Gregory was when they hired him four years before. Let me repeat that—*four years before.*

He had been planning his whole scam on me (and Cathy) for four years. His official goal was to get Mutual to convert, but, if his plan had worked, he would have gotten to convert a couple of girls himself in the process. He'd planned every detail—right down to the unicorn, which he borrowed from Eileen's ranch, where she was taking care of a couple of "magical" creatures. I never would have guessed she was telling the truth about that when she told me about that at the armory on the day I first met Gregory. Most of her creatures really were just things like cats with wings glued to their backs, but still. Who knew?

We thought we were getting a great deal when she offered us five hundred bucks each for the rights to our story.

The council decided to let Mutual's parents live, to Mutual's relief (they were his parents, after all), but they revoked permission for the diciotto, and banished them both to Alaska until further notice—probably as long as Mutual and I are alive.

We haven't heard from them since, which is fine with us.

Mutual had no trouble with any of the standardized tests and GED exams we signed him up for, and pretty soon he was accepted at Drake, too. With a scholarship that someone had set up for the children of vampires.

Murray gave him a summer job in his office and paid him enough that he was able to get himself a tiny little studio apartment, where he spent his free time discovering all the music and movies the rest of us already knew about.

He made some missteps along the way. One day he was all excited over this new kind of music some joker had told him about—it was called "elevator wave," or "mallcore," and turned out to be Muzak—the kind of crud they play at low volume in stores so that you'll buy stuff to relieve the boredom.

And the week he discovered *Maxim* magazine was not my favorite week, either.

But I was with him as much as I possibly could be. I had been so buried in my studies for most of my life that I was way behind in my pop culture education, too. I hadn't even seen *The Princess Bride* until one night when Amber brought it over to Mutual's house. How in the heck could I have missed that?

See? It's not that I hate princess stuff or anything—I liked *Princess Diaries* pretty well, too. I just hate *crappy* princess stuff. And princess stuff that leads people to camp out on my lawn, ready to give up democracy in order to have a servant to scrub their toilets for them.

But, anyway, the point is that it wasn't like Mutual and I rode off into the sunset to live in a castle that we never had to clean or anything.

We argued a lot at first. Sometimes it seemed like Mutual was growing apart from me, or I was growing apart from him, while we figured out what kind of people we were going to be. And the general pressure of all the book stuff, after that came out, really got to us now and then. It's really tough to build a relationship when you have to tell the press that your boyfriend is actually a guy named Fred the vampire (who, in reality, is dead) just to keep him from getting hate mail.

But we've made it work, so far.

And we hadn't argued in weeks as of the night we were all in the limo together, going to the movie premiere.

"This was a bad idea," I said. "We shouldn't have come out here."

"Hey, free limo ride," said Mutual. "I always wanted to ride in one of these things."

"I feel like a complete tool," said Jason.

"They're probably going to boo your character all through the movie, Mutual," I said. "They all think you're a total dork who was stalking me."

"Well, I did kind of send you postcards for years and travel across the country and risk my life for you," he said. "That's kind of stalking."

I laughed and kissed him on the cheek.

Even if we don't end up together, I'll always have a bond with him that I can't imagine having with anyone else. With all of them, really.

"Just ignore them," Amber said. "They won't know you're you. They'll just think you're Fred, as usual."

"I should have worn my gorilla suit," he said. "We all should have."

Even after his parents were no longer a threat, he had still been into the idea that he should get a gorilla suit. Don't ask me why—he just had a thing about them. So he got one.

And then I got one, too. It's not nearly as effective as I'd hoped for running people off the lawn (trust me, you need a bodyguard for that, not a gorilla suit), but when we both get stressed out from all the crap going on, we put on our gorilla suits and run around screaming and beating our chests and throwing bananas around.

It's insanely fun. It's even more cathartic than breaking stuff, and with none of the guilt trip or worries that you're a maniac. You might have to worry that you look like a nut, but you know what? I don't particularly care.

I can't possibly dance naked in front of a window, what with the photographers and all. But I can go jumping around in a gorilla suit, which is sort of the same thing, in a way, if you think about it.

Anyway, as I started college, the future looked bright. Even with the guilt I felt about Fred and Cathy and everything, I remember those as happy days, when everything in the world seemed possible for us.

Then, of course, Eileen's book came out and everything kind of went to hell.

I had to learn to deal with people discussing my weight online, and finding ways to protect my friends' privacy as well as I could. I needed cash, and fast, to pay for security and stuff, which is why I said I was a real princess on some of those talk shows. Sorry I lied. I promise you that I would have preferred to earn money by dropping bowling balls on my toes.

I don't think I can even describe the things I fantasized about happening to Eileen Codlin. I wasn't fantasizing about that stuff as much—being present when Gregory was torn to pieces sort of spoiled my appetite for destruction—but I made exceptions in Eileen's case now and then.

And now the movie version of the book was opening, which I couldn't imagine was going to help me much. I'd probably be more famous than ever. My best hope was that I'd get more expensive—like, I could just make one commercial for something I didn't really think anyone should buy, instead of six or seven.

So now we were in a limo, cruising through the streets of Los Angeles, on the way to the premiere of the movie version of *Born to Be Extraordinary—Jenny's Fairy Godmother*. I hadn't really intended to see the movie at all, but they offered us a free limo ride, a four-star meal, plane tickets to Los Angeles, and all kinds of cool stuff to get us out here. No one who's lived through an Iowa winter would skip a free chance to go to California in the middle of one.

Also, it sounded like too perfect an opportunity for mischief to pass up.

And the limo was pretty nice. I'd been in one a couple of times before, when people flew me out for talk shows and stuff. I'd always felt like a tool in them myself, honestly, but having my friends there made it a lot more fun.

Especially knowing what we were planning to do on the red carpet.

If I was going to have to be famous, at least I could be famous on my own terms, more or less.

I got on the intercom and put in a call to Jared, my bodyguard, who was in the front seat.

Yeah. I have a bodyguard now.

"Just want to give you a heads-up, Jared," I said. "This is gonna be a little different from a day in Des Moines."

"Roger that," said Jared. "You guys planning something?"

"Yes, yes we are," I said.

"I'm going to have to request that you give me all the details," he said.

"Negative," I said. "You'd just try to stop us."

It's awkward having a person working for you—not as weird as having a servant scrubbing my toilet and making my bed would be, but awkward. I like Jared, though. It's hard not to like a guy who will beat people up for you. I totally get that. When girls say they love the Fred in the book because he turns out to be a good protector, I understand where they're coming from.

But I couldn't let him know what we had in mind.

We'd thought about just making armpit noises at appropriate moments during the movie or something, but we decided to go for something bigger.

"Are you sure they aren't going to boo me?" asked Cathy. "If anyone boos me, I'll run."

"No one knows what you look like," I told her. "They all think you're a blonde. You'll be fine."

I thought it would be awfully traumatic for Cathy to find out that she wasn't *really* going to die if Fred didn't kiss me at the dance, and that she didn't *need* to let Gregory . . . do what he did to her. But she took it pretty well. She's in counseling and all, but she's tough. She's a survivor.

In fact, she adapted to life as part of the undead pretty quickly. She was perfectly happy as a vampire for a while there, before Eileen's book came out and all the hate mail started coming.

So leave her alone, guys. She's been through enough. She was never the head of a *Mean Girls*–type clique; we didn't really even have one of those at my school. She was just kind of mean to me, and she's apologized about a million times. I even have coffee with her now and then. We're both Gregory Grue survivors.

It's the kind of thing that makes people feel like there's sort of a bond between them, even if they never got along before. Like nearly getting kicked out of town over a spelling bee, or destroying homecoming with a Wells Fargo Wagon full of unicorn poop.

The limo pulled up to Grauman's Chinese Theatre, and we stepped out onto a red carpet, where Eileen was signing autographs.

"Jenny V!" she shouted when she saw me. "And the whole gang!"

"There's Fred!" someone shouted, pointing at Mutual.

People who really do the research can always find out the truth about Fred and Mutual without too much trouble, but it's amazing how little research people do.

I walked up to Eileen as cordially as possible, holding hands with Mutual all the way.

"Hi, Eileen," I said.

A reporter came up to us.

"So, this is the *real* Princess Jenny, right?" he asked.

"Yes it is!" said Eileen. "The girl who was born to be extraordinary! Isn't this extraordinary, being here tonight, Jenny?"

"Yes it is," I said, as regally as I could, even though I was trying very hard not to laugh, since I knew what was coming.

"So, you are *really* a princess, right?" asked the reporter.

"Yes," I said, "and one of the reasons it's extraordinary to be here tonight is that it's a very special night in my kingdom."

"Oh, really?" the reporter said. "Tell us about it."

I snuck a glance at Eileen, who was nodding as though she knew what I was talking about, though the look in her eyes was something along the lines of "What the hell are you *doing*?"

"Tonight is the night known as Feasteus Maximus," I said. "Which is also known as National Show Your Butt Day. Jason, will you please demonstrate how it's celebrated?"

"With pleasure," said Jason.

And he showed his tattoo to the whole world.

Luckily, some photographer got a picture of the look on Eileen's face. You've seen that picture. The one where Jason's got his butt out and Eileen looks like a kid in a candy store.

That was why we went to the red carpet. We couldn't get a happily-ever-after out of the story, but we could at least get pictures of Eileen swooning over Jason's hairy butt.

The plan kind of backfired, really. I thought we'd just give Jason a chance to do his favorite thing, then maybe coerce Eileen into mooning the crowd, too (Amber and Mutual were both prepared to pitch in, though, as royalty, I was exempt). We didn't anticipate that when word spread about the holiday, things would get way out of control.

So, as part of the settlement with the City of Los Angeles, I'm required to say right now that we were behaving very irresponsibly on the red carpet.

But it was totally worth it. The look on Eileen's face alone was worth the community service and the fight I had to put up to keep my scholarship.

There were other moments that made the trip worth it, too.

Like the after-party, when we said that in my kingdom, we don't *eat* the kind of cheese you get on trays, you *suck* on it. We never did get Eileen to celebrate Feasteus Maximus, but she did demonstrate the proper way to eat cheese. That's why there are also all those pictures of Eileen sucking cheese.

So that's the real story of me, Cathy, Fred, Mutual, my friends, my fairy godmofo, and how I got my wishes.

It's not the way Eileen told the story at all, but the real world just isn't like the world in her book. It's scarier, stinkier, sadder, and stranger. Harder and more dangerous, too. But it's also the kind of world where throwing unicorn poo around a gym can make you feel beautiful. That counts for something, or I don't know what does. It's the kind of world where you can be extraordinary without any magic spell to make you that way. Without even being royalty.

I'm not a princess. But sometimes, like that night when we looked out over the ocean and Mutual told me he loved me for the first time, I sure feel like one.

So there you have it. The real story.

Now get off my lawn.

ADAM SELZER was born in Des Moines and now lives in Chicago, where he writes humorous books for young readers by day and runs ghost tours by night. (If you can find two cooler jobs than those, take them!) He is the author of *I Kissed a Zombie, and I Liked It*; *The Smart Aleck's Guide to American History*; *Andrew North Blows Up the World*; *I Put a Spell on You*; *Pirates of the Retail Wasteland*; and *How to Get Suspended and Influence People*, and he is just famous enough to have a page on Wikipedia. Check him out on the Web at adamselzer.com.